GW00391355

Of All Days

Lily Baines

© 2021 Lily Baines. All rights reserved.

No portion of this book may be reproduced in any form
without permission from the publisher, except as
permitted by U.S. copyright law.

This is a work of fiction. Names, characters, places, and
incidents either are the products of the author's
imagination or are used fictitiously. Any resemblance to
actual persons, living or dead, businesses, companies,
events, or locales is entirely coincidental.

ISBN: 979-850-315-6485

Chapter 1

She'd had it all planned weeks in advance, down to the last detail of what she would wear. But, when the moment came, Olivia Duncan's plans were as effective as the Titanic's promise for a second voyage.

Olivia clutched her laptop backpack closer to her chest as the taxi approached the front of the luxurious conference hotel. She had been preparing for this moment for months, and now she was finally here. But sweaty and frumpy after twenty-four hours of airports and airplanes, of sleeping on uncomfortable benches, of delayed flights, running through endless corridors, and missing a flight, wasn't how she had planned her arrival at Corfu.

The night air was warm when Olivia climbed out of the taxi and shouldered her only piece of luggage. She could smell the nearby sea right before she was swallowed up by the large, brightly illuminated building.

"I'm sorry, the town's shops closed at nine, but the hotel boutique is still open for the next half hour. You can try there," the girl at the front desk responded in reply to Olivia's inquiry, smiling sympathetically. "I'll let you know if your suitcase arrives, but it's more than likely that the airline will contact you directly."

"Thank you," Olivia mumbled, taking the room's card key.

At the hotel's boutique, which was a fancy name for a simple gift shop that contained a hybrid of pool inflatables, beachwear, graphic T-shirts, ugly coral jewels, sunscreen, and basic toiletries, Olivia had lost all hope.

She bought a white "*I heart Greece*" tee because it was the least horrid in the collection that hung on the store's clothing rack. She hoped it would be considered endearing if she gave her keynote presentation the next morning wearing it instead of her specially-bought pencil-skirt grey suit that was somewhere in transit inside her lost suitcase.

After buying a few must-have toiletries, she went up to the room.

Spacious and clean, though somewhat impersonal, as hotel rooms tend to be, it had a comfortable bed and a fully equipped bathroom. One look in the mirror made Olivia realize that she wouldn't be able to restore the sleek, professionally done bob that she had left Seattle with, even if she used the poorly powered blow dryer that hung on the bathroom wall.

After a relaxing shower and a little panic attack when her tired mind grasped that her makeup kit and contact lenses were also inside her suitcase, Olivia crawled into the big bed and let the cool, soft sheets hug her into sleep.

~~~~~~~~~~~~~~~~~~~~~~~~~~~~~~~~~~

The alarm she'd had enough brain capacity to set the night before woke her up at seven a.m. and, by five minutes to eight, Olivia stood on the stage at the conference room, connecting her laptop to the large screen while the attendees took their seats.

She was as ready as she could be, despite having to wear the wrinkly pair of jeans that she had flown in. If she blew the audience off with her well-prepared presentation, they wouldn't mind her inappropriate clothes, the fact that her natural ash-slash-mousey-blonde hair frizzed like parsley, or that she looked washed out with no makeup and large-framed eyeglasses. Besides, at breakfast that morning, she had resolved herself to preface her presentation with a joke so that everyone would understand why she looked like a hobo who had snuck into a Nobel prize ceremony.

But, two hours later, sitting at a side table in what seemed like a locals-only taverna at the other side of Corfu, Olivia watched the videos of herself that had been uploaded by multiple people to Twitter. Some were hash-tagged *#ConferenceFail* and, in all of them, she looked pitiful in her "*I heart Greece*" shirt and the shabby ensemble that accompanied it. Most pitiful of all was the *I want to die* expression on her face as she read along with the three-hundred attendees the instant message that popped up on the large screen right before her speech.

Sprinkled with eggplant and tongue emojis, for good measure, the message had read:

> *Oh, come on, Livvy; you haven't gotten a decent orgasm in months, maybe years. And when was the last time Jeff had gone down there? You're well rid of him, and I hope you get laid on this trip by some hot*

Greek guy or at least by that cute one from TechCell. Remember the motto: Don't give head before you get one. Love ya, babe! Good luck! Good lay!

To make matters worse, the message had half-covered her opening slide, titled:

Giving Tech A Head Start
Day 1
Welcome by Olivia Duncan, HR Consultant for DoITmore

Until that moment, she had thought her title very apt. But, along with the name of the company that she had represented, it received a whole different connotation next to the instant messaging app that had jumped up automatically to reveal Daria's message to her. She couldn't even hide in anonymity; her full name had been on display and cherry-topped the options for public humiliation.

Olivia placed the phone facedown on the table. Daria's multiple apologetic texts and unanswered calls from her manager, colleagues, and mother all awaited. She had managed to read just two messages. "*Don't open Twitter*," from her brother, and, "*Sweetie, I'm so sorry. I swear I'll make it up to you. Don't go into Twitter*," from Daria.

Olivia stared blankly through the window at the deserted village street, wondering if there were films of her disconnecting her computer from the screen and saying, "Good morning. Enjoy the conference," in a lowered, flushed face, avoiding everyone's eyes, before she had run out of the room.

She had gotten into the first taxi outside the hotel and had asked the driver to take her as far as possible to the other side of the island, preferably to a non-touristic spot. The village where he had dropped her off, forty minutes later, wasn't directly on a beach and looked sleepy and rustic. It had charm, but not as much as the amazing views of the island that she had seen on the way there.

Wandering along its only main square and street, she had noticed the *Teresi Taverna* sign but had felt too devastated to sit in one place. Instead, she had strolled the side alleys for a while.

Unlike postcards of Greek islands, this village had more than white houses with blue shutters and white-washed cobbles. Google had told her when she had prepared for this trip that only the Cyclades islands had those white views, but Corfu was an Ionian island. From the little she had managed to see of it, it was dominated by colorful houses, lush green hills, and the turquoise sea and beaches were seen from almost every spot.

"Hi, do you have coffee? Preferably a strong one," she now asked the handsome local who manned the bar at the taverna.

"*Kalimera*," he greeted a good morning, sliding his gaze to her "*I heart Greece*" T-shirt. "No English," he added.

Olivia bit her upper lip. She desperately needed something strong, and although she craved the tranquility that the quaint Teresi Taverna offered and didn't want to speak to anyone, she wanted to be understood enough to order something comforting for her churning stomach.

"Coffee. Café?" she tried again, hoping this would help when the man's face remained blank.

This, he seemed to understand. He nodded, and a small glass of black, aromatic coffee landed on her window table not long after. He served it himself with a side of a small glass of water, a dip bowl filled with olives, and a charming, lopsided smile. Even in her state, she noticed the contours of a good body under his black, button-down shirt, with sleeves folded to reveal strong, tan forearms.

Five or six sips were enough to get her through the small cup, and an unwelcome surprise in the shape of the grinds filling her mouth and throat caused Olivia to cough. Instinctively, she picked up the water glass and gulped its content down before the acute licorice smell and taste revealed that it was ouzo.

Coughing, her eyes tearing up, she looked over at the bar and saw the man gleefully smiling and waving at her.

"Thanks a lot, dickhead," she muttered between coughs, removing her plastic-framed eyeglasses to wipe her eyes. She didn't think he could hear her but was glad all the same that he didn't understand English and wouldn't be affected by the word that she had let slip.

Putting the eyeglasses back on, Olivia noticed that his smile had widened and he nodded at her. She fake-smiled back before moving to gaze through the window at the street with its sparse traffic of vehicles and people. The drink now sent warm waves from her stomach to the rest of her body. It was surprisingly soothing.

This trip was supposed to be her well-earned prize. Surviving her boss's tendency to take credit for her work, Olivia had finally been given the opportunity to present her two-year project at the *When Human Resources Meets Engineering* conference. It didn't matter that she had been chosen to represent their consultancy agency only after her manager, Doreen, had realized the conference wouldn't fit her planned wedding date and thus wouldn't be able to honeymoon in Greece with the flights paid for by the agency.

"The conference isn't until June; why are you working on this four months in advance?" Doreen had asked before leaving the office one evening.

"It'll be my first time presenting abroad. I want it to be perfect," Olivia had replied. For months, she had fine-tuned her slides, rehearsed them, prepared and coordinated every detail.

Her split from Jeff after ten years had been the first glitch in her plan for an immaculate execution. That had ironically made the expected trip to Greece especially welcome.

The phone buzzed repeatedly on the table and shook Olivia back to reality. Daria's name flashed on the screen.

Hesitating but pitying her best friend who was probably too mortified to sleep, even though it was one a.m. in Seattle, Olivia picked up the call.

"I'm so sorry, Livvy! I didn't know this thing would jump up on your screen. I'm *sorry*. You were so looking forward to this. Will you ever forgive me?" The barrage of words, spoken in a shriek, had Olivia distance the phone from her ear.

"It's okay. You couldn't have known. How did it circle to you that fast, though? Twitter?"

"Oh, sweetie, rumors fly fast." Daria worked for a Seattle-based, high-tech company that had many joint acquaintances. "Besides, there's … yes, videos on Twitter. I'm *so* sorry."

"I've seen a few."

"Oh no, honey, I'm sorry. Promise me you won't go in there again."

"I will, eventually." Olivia sighed. "Don't feel bad. This whole trip was a disaster from start to finish. The flight from New York was delayed for hours, which made me miss the internal flight from Athens to Corfu, so I arrived less than twelve hours before the conference opening. Then my luggage never arrived, and I had to buy this stupid T-shirt at the hotel store. Everything, including my contacts, was in that suitcase, and … I bought a bikini bottom because I didn't have clean panties, and that's what I slept in, and this is what I'm wearing now under these ugly flight jeans."

"Oh no, sweetie! I am so, so sorry. I wish I could do something. Can I do something?" Daria sounded on the verge of tears.

"No. Nothing. Really. I have to get clean clothes, and I have to call Doreen back. I wish you could call her for me and tell her that … I don't know, I fell off a cliff here."

"Are you still at the hotel?"

"No, I left. Didn't those bastards film that, too? I couldn't stay there."

"Where are you now?"

"I don't know … Some hole on a mountain here, in a taverna that serves unfiltered coffee with alcohol before noon."

"You could use alcohol before noon today," Daria said and, despite the situation, they both chuckled.

Olivia cut her laughter short. It was too close to turning into tears.

"I wish I could be there to hug you. I feel so bad, honey," Daria added.

"Nah, it's not your fault. I thought I had the app disabled, but I guess my computer crashing then rebooting—which, by the way, also happened while I was between flights—canceled my previous settings." Olivia sighed. "I hope Jeff didn't see it."

"What if he did? I hope he takes notes. I should have used less … colorful words, but I meant what I wrote. Your relationship was on life support for years. Nothing to regret."

"I didn't say I regretted it."

"If he gets over himself, he'll probably send you one of his vanilla, internet quotes." It used to drive Daria crazy whenever Jeff had sent Olivia inspirational stickers and quotes. "It was cute at first, but ten years later, you realize he just doesn't have anything to say. It's better to shut up and hug someone than send them a picture of a mountain with a quote when they need you," she had said when such a picture had landed in Olivia's phone when she had lost a promotion to a colleague.

Olivia sighed. "All true, but he's a good guy." She could use a good guy right now, vanilla and all.

"I know, but no one can live only on vanilla for ten years. And you, my friend, almost lost your taste buds. So, he did you a favor. Why don't you use your time there to do something fun, to restart?"

"I'll probably be asked to be on the first flight out of here and report to management. They won't want me here."

"Do you forgive me?"

"There's nothing to forgive. Now, go to bed—it's late there—and don't worry about me. I'll drown my sorrow in more of that ouzo they serve here."

"Okay, hon. Call me and keep me posted."

"I will. Bye."

The taverna was empty now, except for her and the bartender, who seemed engulfed in his cell phone.

Olivia took her bag and went to the bar. "Excuse me. Bathroom?" she asked, hoping he would get it.

He raised a pair of honey-green eyes to her, then pointed at a door to the far right.

She wished she remembered how to say "thank you" in Greek. Instead, she muttered it in English.

After relieving herself from the coffee and washing her face in the sink, Olivia ran wet fingers through her unruly hair, trying to subdue the puffy cloud that hovered over her head. She had more bad hair days than she cared to remember. Being stranded on a hot Greek island with sea air and humidity, and no blow dryer or her products, meant a bad hair era, not day.

"Is there a hotel here?" she inquired after returning to the bar. "Bed and breakfast? Room?" Just the thought of going back to the hotel with everyone who had witnessed and contributed to her humiliation made her want to really jump off a cliff. She would hide here until she could find a flight. Good thing she hadn't left any belongings behind. Her laptop was in her backpack, which she had taken with her when she had escaped.

"A room? Hotel?" she repeated, leaning her cheek sideways on her pressed palms and closing her eyes for a moment in what she hoped was the universal sign for sleep.

She pushed back an exasperated sigh when the man just returned her gaze. Then, frustrated, knowing that he didn't understand, anyway, she said without taking her eyes off him, "How come you don't know English? Never left this village?"

He continued to eye her, then smiled that charming smile again.

"At least you've got *that* going for you," she muttered, tapping her phone and opening Google Translate. She quickly typed her question into it and, as the translation into Greek appeared, she turned her screen toward him. His eyes were intent on her before he moved to read the message. He then shook his head.

"No hotel?" She was desperate. It was beyond her current strength to look for another village, another place.

Starting to feel uncomfortable under his scrutiny, she smoothed a hand over her hair, then pushed her eyeglasses back to their place. Under his dark, wavy, short hair, he had a face that matched the fantasy women had of Greek men. It made her even more aware of her own uncomely state.

They continued to gaze at each other.

"This dickhead doesn't think this mountain hole has accommodations that will satisfy you."

Olivia jerked her head back. The words were spoken in clear English with a sexy accent overtaking his somewhat raspy voice.

Chapter 2

"So, you *do* speak English? Why did you pretend not to?" Anger mixed with embarrassment bubbled inside her. Of all days, this wasn't a day she could deal with pranks at her expense.

"We try to keep this village tourists-free."

"On purpose? How noble."

"Not noble. We just want our peace and quiet."

"Isn't tourism a good business?"

"Money can't buy peace and quiet."

Their gazes on each other, Olivia concluded that all that mattered right now was a place to hide in until she could go back home.

She cleared her throat and broke eye contact. "Anyway, it did sound like there's a place here where people can stay. Is there?"

The man continued to eye her. "Not exactly," he said after a moment's hesitation.

"Listen, I may be a tourist, but I'm not looking for something fancy or touristy."

"With this T-shirt, I thought I knew your kind." His tone somewhat softened.

"It's a long story." She hoped he wouldn't hold her previous attitude against her. She wasn't her usual self. Then again, he was far from blameless.

"Yes, I sort of heard. You weren't exactly silent on the phone."

"And you still pretended you didn't know English."

He pressed his lips together and raised his brows, tilting his head in a *yep, sorry* gesture. "I did that before I heard. I'm sorry about that. Calling me a name didn't land you on my best side."

She rubbed a hand between her eyebrows. "It hasn't been a very good day for me so far. I'm sorry I called you—"

"A dickhead," he completed for her.

"Yes, that. Sorry. I don't usually … And it's not a mountain hole; it's beautiful, and I like that it's somewhat secluded."

He smiled. It was more bewitching when it reached his eyes. She noticed the age lines at the sides of his mouth and eyes and estimated he was about her age—late thirties.

"What?" she asked.

"You complimented my village now and my smile before, so I forgive you."

She smiled back. "Well, I haven't forgiven *you* yet for pretending not to know English and having a go at me with that coffee and ouzo."

"This coffee is something you should expect here. So is the ouzo." He reached his hand over the bar. "Niko."

Surprised, she extended hers. He took it in a strong grip of a large and used-to-manual-work palm.

"I'm Olivia, nice to meet you."

They gazed at each other.

"So, Niko, is there a place here I can stay?"

He breathed out. "Like I said, not exactly. There's … a vacant house two streets away."

"If it has furniture, I'll take it. I just need it for two nights or so. Can you tell me where it is?"

"It's furnished, it's clean, but it's not supposed to be a B&B."

"That's okay. Just give me the address. I can find it."

"There are no exact addresses here. It'd be easier if I took you there." His English was surprisingly good, and his accent rolled the words softly on his tongue.

"Can you take me there now?" She hadn't seen any other staff there but had heard noises coming from the kitchen, passing by it on the way to the restroom.

"In a few minutes. Go sit, and I'll bring you another Greek coffee. Be careful when you finish it this time."

She huffed a little, dry chuckle as she went back to her seat.

Niko made a phone call, and she heard him speak in Greek while he served her coffee.

A few minutes later, an older man entered the place and went behind the bar. He and Niko exchanged a few words, and the man looked at her.

"Let's go," Niko called over to her.

She picked up her bag and hurried toward him.

"Olivia, this is my uncle, Kostas."

"*Kalimera*." She had recalled the local greeting, and the man, who reminded her of the bold and mustached restauranteur from *Lady and The Tramp*, greeted her back with a longer expression that she didn't understand.

Stepping outside, the bright sun was blinding after the shade of the taverna. Olivia wished she had her sunglasses with her.

Following Niko's determined, slightly bowlegged stride, she estimated him to be six-foot tall, as every step he took required almost two of her own.

"There's a clothing shop at the next village down there." He pointed at another cluster of houses not far below them on the hillside. "There's a bus that stops here every two hours. You can take it there."

"Thank you." She stifled an embarrassed, nervous chuckle, realizing he had heard enough of her conversation with Daria to know what she wore in lieu of panties.

He greeted a few people they passed by who gazed at her curiously. Olivia nodded at them, feeling like she was on display for the second time that day.

Coming down a narrow, curvy alley with houses on both sides, they turned a corner into a row of houses built on the side of the hill, bordering the open view around and beneath them. The two-story, colorful houses were dotted with even more colorful bougainvilleas, flowerbeds, and hanging flower pots. At the end of the row stood a peach-colored one-story house with green, wooden shutters. With an open veranda overlooking a breathtaking view of the grove that sloped below and the sea in the distance, the little house looked like something right out of a postcard.

"Is this it?" she asked as Niko made his way toward it, breaking the silence between them.

"Yes."

To complete the picture, a set of white, wrought-iron ornamented garden chairs and a table with a blue, white, and peach mosaic top stood on the veranda and a vine climbed up the columns that supported it. It was a much more welcome sight than the huge and overly sophisticated hotel she had escaped from.

"Very beautiful. Peaceful," she commented.

"Yes, it is." He extracted a key from the pocket of his black jeans.

"Is it *yours*?"

"My family's."

"So, there's a taverna and this beautiful place to let, and yet you try to repel tourists?" She addressed the question at his broad back, stopping to stand behind him at the green, wooden front door.

"It's not a place to let, and most tourists don't come here, anyway," he replied, busy with the lock. "We don't have noisy nightlife or busy beaches." He pushed the door open, then turned to look at her.

"Wow." The word escaped her lips as she followed him into a bright space that combined a living room and a kitchen, and a large glass door that connected those with the veranda. The sunlight washed in through the closed white curtains that matched the warm, light, relaxing colors of the room. The furniture seemed plain but comfortable. The kitchen looked like that of a home with pots and pans hanging over a light blue wooden island.

"Two bedrooms and a bathroom over there." Niko pointed, and she went to peek into the rooms. They matched the rest of the house, looking clean, spacious, and comfortable.

"You said two nights, right?" he asked when she met him in the living space again.

"Yes, just until I get a flight. Will that be okay?"
He nodded once.

"How much do I owe you?" she asked.

His jaw muscle twitched. "It's free."

"What? No, come on; I want to pay." She hadn't planned for accommodation expenses during that disastrous trip, but it was the better option. Even going back home to face everything wasn't that alluring at the moment, especially not her half-empty apartment with some of her belongings still packed in boxes that collected dust in the corner of her bedroom on the third floor of her new building.

"I told you, it's not usually for rent."

"Okay, but …"

"We'll talk about this later," Niko said, handing her the key. He then smiled. "No breakfast service here, but you can come to the taverna and get one. There's also a grocery store on the main street. Oh, and no cleaning service."

Olivia let out a tired chuckle. "That's okay. Thank you."

"Enjoy your stay, I guess." His tone made it sound like a question, which made sense given her unusual circumstances. "I hope you won't hate Greece." He jutted his chin toward her shirt, smirking.

"Thanks." Her smile was faint.

~~~~~~~~~~~~~~~~~~~~~~~~~~~~~~~~

After he left, Olivia stepped out onto the veranda and breathed in the clear air and the view. She could almost forget how her much-anticipated day had begun. But she didn't have the luxury of forgetting, not when her phone was filled with unanswered calls, texts, and alerts. To postpone the moment of facing those, she decided to walk toward the next village to buy clothes and get rid of those she had on.

Few cars drove by as Olivia made her way down the narrow-laned asphalt that led from one village to the next. Turning her head to look back at the road sign, she discovered the name of the village she was staying in. "*Aleniki*," she read out loud.

Despite the breeze and some shade provided by the oak, cypress, and olive trees, Olivia was sweating by the time she reached the bigger and busier village below.

Closer to the beach, it boasted several shops and tavernas in its main square, and B&B signs hung on many houses. Fragments of English and German reached her ears as she passed by vacationers. Olivia shuddered involuntarily, though no one here knew her.

Twenty minutes after finding the clothing shop, she was the proud owner of a pack of six panties, one bra, a pair of unbranded blue jeans, four shirts, two summer dresses, and a pair of red sandals that had caught her eyes. It wasn't as smart as what she had packed at home, but it was better than wearing the same clothes and shoes for over twenty-four hours. To be on the safe side, she had bought enough to last her in case she couldn't find a seat on the next flight out.

In a nearby tiny drugstore, she bought essential toiletries to replace those she had left in the hotel room. She couldn't find contact lenses or makeup, except for a rose-tinted Chapstick, which she bought.

This time, she took the bus back. After a long shower, still wrapped in a big white towel that she had found in a closet, Olivia made the bed in one of the bedrooms, using beddings that she had obtained from the same closet. Soon after, she fell asleep, the white curtains of the west-facing window above the bed flying in the afternoon sea breeze.

The endless buzzing of her phone on the nightstand jolted Olivia out of a dream. Confused, she looked around until everything came back to her. The sky outside glowed in a mix of orange and purple.

A quick glance at the screen proved that it was almost eight p.m. and that she had two missed calls from her manager and several other text messages from various people.

After replying with a "*Don't worry, I'm ok*," to her brother, mother, and Daria, she made herself a cup of coffee from ground beans that she found in the kitchen. Strengthened by the warm drink and watching the glow the sun had left over the sea from the veranda, Olivia felt she could cope with Doreen.

In a new, deep-blue shift dress that matched the color of her eyes, and her shoulder-length hair under control, she withstood her manager's barely screened criticism.

"We all agree that it wasn't your fault, but surely, you understand that it's not a very good representation of, or reflection on, our brand."

"You *all* agreed?"

"Surely, you can imagine that an urgent meeting was called first thing this morning with all the relevant stakeholders."

"Surely," Olivia retorted.

"DoITmore wants to cancel their contract with us."

For the first time since that morning, tears stung the back of Olivia's eyes. DoITmore was her account and, for two years, she had worked to measurably increase their engineers' innovation by improving their HR programs. That was what she had come to present at the conference.

"I didn't write that message. It was a private message from a friend that unfortunately popped up."

"We know, but it made many people uncomfortable."

Anger was added to the mix of humiliation and shame that clogged Olivia's throat. Her heart raced in her chest, and her voice came out hoarse. "So uncomfortable that several of them took their phones out to film it and post it on social media?"

"Yes, well … We have to focus on protecting our brand now."

With Doreen insisting on "*we*," Olivia knew she was being abandoned on the battlefield.

"What do you want me to do now?" She just wanted this nightmare to end.

"Book a flight back, and we'll talk about what's next when you're here."

Olivia had been in this line of work long enough to know that that wording didn't bear any good news for her upon her return.

"Okay," came out as a whisper.

Her manager had not one word of sympathy for her, not an ounce of real understanding. She had worked for Teamtastic Consultancy for a decade, always excelling at her job, moving from an assistant role to an account manager, then working closely with Doreen, the HR consultancy unit manager. She had executed several large projects where most of the credit had gone to Doreen, who had gotten to present them at conferences. However, she believed in what they did and had stuck with it.

Or maybe she was stuck in it. Ten years in the agency, and the same number with Jeff, whom she had met there before he had moved to work in another firm. Now, at the age of thirty-eight, she was back to square one. No relationship and, from the sound of it, no career, either.

Chapter 3

Olivia had to clear her head from all this. Or fuzz it up. Both could work.

Going out into the quiet alleys that were now blanketed in the scented, warm night air, she was all alone. Her friends and family were a sea, an ocean, and two continents away. The only people she knew here were Niko and Kostas, and neither seemed too friendly. At least here she enjoyed anonymity. No one in this village, except Niko, knew about her public humiliation, and even he didn't know the details from the little he had overheard.

The main street, which hardly measured up in width or length to a suburban street in Seattle, was fully lit. String lights hung over it, and the trees were decorated with fairy lights, giving everything a festive look. Several people were seated around tables outside the taverna. Warm, welcoming lights wafted from it and onto the street. From a distance, it reminded Olivia of Van Gogh's *Café Terrace At Night*, which was the only framed picture that hung on her new apartment's wall. That poster, bought in an exhibition that she had visited with Daria during the first year of their graduate degree, had accompanied her in every apartment move since.

There were four occupied tables inside, and the music of the language revealed that the people around them were all local. Olivia looked across at the bar. Niko, in a button-down blue shirt, its sleeves folded to his elbows, was busy filling glasses.

Looking around, she decided to sit at the small window table that she had earlier. The nausea she had been sporting all day gave way to hunger. She hadn't eaten since the croissant that she'd had right before the calamitous conference.

A menu was written in chalk on the wall behind the bar, but all Olivia could read were the prices. The rest was in the Greek alphabet.

Niko, serving drinks to a nearby table, spotted her and nodded in recognition. "*Kalispera*," he greeted a good evening upon reaching her.

"Oh, *Kalispera*."

"Found everything okay?" A fresh, watery scent of soap and aftershave wafted from him.

"Yes, absolutely. Thank you so much for letting me stay there. Thought I'd eat something here tonight, but I can't read the menu." She smiled.

"Yes, sorry, we didn't expect any tourists here." His tone and expression conveyed amusement. "I'll ask Elena to bring you a bit from everything, and you can decide."

"I'm vegetarian."

He huffed a dry chuckle. "Okay, so a bit of half of what we have."

"Sounds good." She couldn't help but chuckle back.

Not long after, an older woman in a flowery dress, under a large, black apron, crossed the terracotta floor from the kitchen, carrying a large tray filled with appetizer-sized plates.

"Meze," the woman said, pointing at the tray. She then named each of the small dishes in Greek, moving her brown eyes between Olivia and the tray, as if to ensure the stranger was following her lesson. The only word Olivia recognized was "tzatziki," which she had become familiar with through Walmart's cucumber dip that she had bought a few times during one of her healthy-eating outbursts.

What awaited on the tray tasted like nothing Olivia had bought back home. The tzatziki was creamy with fresh dill, cucumbers, and a hint of garlic. The various fresh or cooked vegetable dishes were delicious in sight, smell, and taste.

On a full stomach and with a lemongrass teacup that Elena had brought, Olivia felt brave enough to venture into social media again. To the constant low hum of people talking at nearby tables, silverware and glasses clinking, and fragments of Greek music in the background, she opened her many notifications on Twitter. The only reason she had kept that profile was to promote Teamtastic. All her tweets were business-related—articles and celebratory mentions of the agency and its clients' success stories.

She nearly choked on her tea.

#DoITmoreOrgasmic was the new hashtag attached to several videos, all featuring the screen with her name, the company's, and Daria's message. Her stomach clenched. With her shocked expression, bad-hair-day coiffe, and inadequate clothing, she did look like her planned little joke that was supposed to defuse the atmosphere—a hobo crashing the Nobel prize ceremony.

Yearning for a glass of wine, Olivia deactivated her Twitter account and shut her phone. She glanced at the bar. Niko leaned against it and spoke to a woman who sat on a high bar stool in front of him. She wore a long, colorful skirt that cascaded from her seat and a white, fitted tank top. Her long, golden-brown hair was smooth down her tanned back. They seemed friendly, and Olivia experienced a strange pinch of jealousy, not at them specifically, but at having someone familiar to talk with intimately.

Jeff was not an option, Daria would be at work at this hour, and the thought of calling her mother stressed Olivia even more. As supportive and loving as Becky Duncan was in her texts, the moment of *how could this happen* would come if Olivia spoke to her.

Her accountant parents were probably cringing at what their friends would think of this scandal. Something like that should never have happened to the daughter who had been the consolation, the balm to their wounded parental pride over the growing pains that her older brother's behavior had given them. Even now, many years after her brother had left behind his difficult years and settled down with a family and an import business, which they had invested in, her parents still treated him with silk gloves for fear that something would go awry, while expecting her to never create as much as a ripple. And she never had.

Top of her high school class, Summa Cum Laude in university, then landing a good job in a respectable company, getting promoted, and maintaining a steady relationship with a software engineer had answered almost all their expectations of her.

The first breach had been her breakup with Jeff, which had seemed just as hard on them as it had been on her. Though Becky and Jack Duncan had supported her decision to not follow Jeff to Boston when he had accepted a job offer there, she had suffered the brunt of their disappointment in him.

"Your job is just as important. He should have thought about that," her mother had said, but Olivia could hear the *why didn't he love you enough* accusation that had hid behind the spoken words. She had postponed telling them about the split until after she had found an apartment and had been able to convince herself that they had *both* eventually chosen their jobs over each other.

She must have been too absorbed in her own thoughts to notice that she was staring at Niko and the woman at the bar. At some point, Niko must have felt her gaze on them, because he suddenly looked over at her and made a gesture of *finished?* with his palms, pointing at her table.

Olivia shuddered out of her reverie, pasted a smile, and nodded.

Niko said something to the woman, then sailed from behind the bar to approach her table.

The woman pivoted on her seat and looked at Olivia. She was beautiful, though her face seemed much older than Olivia had expected, given her figure, hair, and clothes.

"How was it? Do you want more of something?" Niko asked, sounding matter of fact.

Olivia didn't mean to, but her eyes were drawn to his hands. No, no ring. She hadn't been wrong about it. "No, thanks. I'm full. Everything was so good. What are these?" She pointed at a leftover bite of something that she had been too full to finish.

"Dolmades. It's vine leaves cooked and stuffed with rice and herbs."

"I liked them!"

Two men from a nearby table, preparing to leave, called Niko's name. He exchanged a few words and a chuckle with them. Olivia enjoyed listening to the melody of the language. To her untrained ear, it sounded like a combination of Spanish and Italian. Niko then brought his eyes back to her.

"Can I get you anything else?"

"Maybe a glass of wine," she said, casting her eyes to the phone that lay facedown on the table.

"Want to try something local?"

"Sure. Why not?"

Niko seemed to hesitate for a moment, which made her lift her eyes and direct them at him.

"Come over to the bar, and I'll let you taste a few things," he said with that half-smile.

It was a bit unexpected, but she was glad to be invited.

Pushing her eyeglasses back up her nose, she said, "Thanks. I'll join you soon."

After using the restroom, Olivia ran a wet hand through her curls to settle them a bit more. Though it frizzed, her hair color hid the white hairs that had appeared over the last few years. Extracting the only makeup she had with her, the Chapstick, she applied it to enliven her naturally pale lips. Her blue, plastic-framed eyeglasses brought out the blue of her eyes and softened the lines that had been added in recent years around her eyes, nose, and mouth.

At the bar, Niko was leaning with his forearms on the counter, absorbed again in a conversation with the pretty, older woman. When Olivia reached them, they broke their conversation, Niko straightened up, and they both looked at her.

"Olivia, this is Thalia."

"Hi." The woman smiled, extending a hand with long fingers and several delicate silver rings.

"Hi, nice to meet you." Olivia shook Thalia's hand.

"You're staying at Niko's house?" Thalia asked with a local accent.

"No. I mean, yes, at the little house he … rents. Not his actual house." Olivia felt her face flushing as Niko and Thalia chuckled.

"No, I know," Thalia said.

"I live above the taverna," Niko explained, looking at Olivia.

She had observed before that there was a second floor to the ochre-painted building and that the balcony above the taverna looked like it belonged to someone's home.

Thalia said something in Greek to Niko, then stood up. "I have to go. Have a good night," she added in English to Olivia.

"I hope she didn't leave on my account," she said after Thalia had left.

"No, no. Don't worry. So, what do you want to start with?"

"I don't know. I trust you."

"Really? After the ouzo for water today?" He had a mischievous smirk on his face.

Olivia laughed.

"Okay. Try this." He placed two glasses on the bar, smaller than normal shot glasses, and filled them with a liquid the color of brandy. "I don't want to get you drunk, so just a tiny amount."

Olivia sniffed it. Niko took one of the glasses and reached it toward hers.

"*Yamas*," he said, then clinked his glass with hers.

"*Yamas*," she cheered back. It tasted like cinnamon and something else. "Wow, I like this one."

"Rakomelo. Made from non-flavored tsipouro with honey, cinnamon, and cardamon. Glad you like it. Try this," he said while pouring a small shot from another bottle. "I use it for cocktails, but tell me what you think." *That accent.*

"*Yamas*." She sipped. "It's sweet. Honey-like, too."

"Mastic liquor," he asserted. "Thought you needed something sweet today."

Their glances met.

"I do. Thank you."

"People can be *malaka*," he said, smiling.

"I don't know what that means, but I have a feeling I'd agree with it."

"It means something like what you called me earlier today."

Olivia laughed and blushed. The alcohol, though in small quantity, was strong and now pleasantly fuzzed her stomach and head. Then again, she was pretty sure it wasn't just the alcohol that made her notice how Niko's shirt fitted his shoulders and arms, revealing a muscular contour, and the glimpse of chest through the top two open buttons made her want to see more of that tan skin that contrasted beautifully with the blue of his shirt.

"Did you find the store?" he asked. She must have looked confused because he then added, "The dress." His gaze quickly skimmed over her dress, or what he could see of it from behind the bar.

"Yes, thanks." It had been a long while since she had been "on the market" and wondered if it was flirtation in his tone and demeanor. It was too matter of fact. She had been used to Jeff's slick hints. And to Jeff's sleek, well-groomed looks. This man was so different with his stubble that looked like a real five o'clock rather than the result of using the designated head of the shaving machine.

Maybe she *should* take Daria's advice, the part that related to finding a hot Greek guy. She felt cocooned in this little village, as if the hotel, the morning, Twitter, and her manager were in a different universe. Things seemed possible. A timeout before she would have to face it all again. Besides, if he had been on that app that Daria had installed on her cell phone, she would definitely swipe him right.

"So, you live upstairs?" she heard herself asking and almost immediately regretted it. It was unlike her. She felt unnatural.

"Yes. My father owned this taverna, and when I took over several years ago, I bought the apartment above it."

He broke eye contact while speaking, and Olivia thought she heard a different tone in his voice. He also seemed to have missed or ignored the hint behind her question, which was just as well.

"Whose house am I staying in now?"

"It's an old family house," he said, disappearing from view for a moment, ducking to put away a tray of used glasses that Elena had just placed on the bar. "I repaired it, almost rebuilt it. Thalia helped decorate it," he added while straightening up. "I stayed in it for a while after I got back to the village, but then I decided to move here." He gestured with his head toward the ceiling.

"Where did you return from?" *And who exactly is Thalia?* she wanted to add.

"Long story," he said, then turned to put things away in the cabinet that stretched along the brick wall beneath the exhibition of bottles and glasses.

Olivia wanted to know more. This place and the life people led here seemed so different than hers. Her tired, drowsy brain wondered, though she knew it couldn't really be, if living here was like in *Mama Mia*—all song and dance, and problems made bearable with this backdrop of gorgeous landscape and solved within an hour and a half.

The taverna was emptying now, but the space still looked warm and welcoming with its soft lights, terracotta floors, and wooden furniture. The open terrace brought in cooler air.

Olivia gazed around at the few pictures with views of the island that hung on the walls.

"Want to try some dessert?" Niko returned to his post at the bar, but his gaze followed, with a smile and a nod, a couple who was exiting.

Olivia watched him, his honey-green eyes and the creases around them, the handsome face with its sculpted angles, and wondered what it was about this small village taverna owner that made her feel like there was much more to him than he let on.

"I probably shouldn't." She tried to keep her eyes on his when he brought his gaze back to her. She wasn't sure why it took an effort. Maybe because it wasn't like her to try to hit on someone, though she wasn't even sure if that was what she had attempted to do. All she knew was that he was nice and attractive, and she'd had a day that was reality's equivalent to those dreams where you stand naked in front of the whole school. She needed comfort, and her usual comforters—Daria, Jeff, even her mother—weren't there. She wasn't the one-night stand type and hadn't been with another man in ten years.

"I think I'll call it a night. My boss asked me to search for a flight, so I have that to do, and I'm still jet-lagged."

Niko nodded, pressing his lips together. He then cleared their glasses and put away the bottles. When he turned back and noticed the credit card that Olivia had placed on the bar, he pushed it toward her. "No need. I'll include it in your room rate."

"But ..."

Elena showing up without her apron and saying something to Niko in Greek had cut Olivia short. He replied to Elena, who ran her fingers through her short, smooth, salt and pepper hair. She then muttered something that sounded like a greeting and left.

"*Kalispera*," Olivia called, hoping that it was still a suitable greeting at that hour of the night.

Niko pushed her credit card further toward her, looking right into her eyes.

"If the house isn't for rent, why did you agree for me to stay in it?"

A small smile flashed across his face then disappeared. "You seemed lost, and it just stands there empty."

Olivia nodded, chewing on her lower lip. "How do you say *thank you*? I memorized all the basics before I left home, but I'm blacking out when I need it."

"*Efkharisto*." He smiled, his eyes glinting, the word rolling out of his mouth.

"*Efkharisto*, Niko," she repeated, failing to mimic his accent. "My room rate is zero, so we're not done talking about this. See you tomorrow," she added, getting to her feet.

"Goodnight, Olivia."

~~~~~~~~~~~~~~~~~~~~~~~~~~~~~~~~~~~~~

A flight with a layover in Amsterdam, two days later, was the closest Olivia found while sitting on the veranda. The lights around, below, and across from her were enchanting. She emailed the details to Doreen, avoiding looking at the long list of emails that had accumulated in her inbox. After texting, "*I'm still ok; don't worry, will be home on Sunday*," to Daria, her mother, and her brother, she shut the laptop down then crashed on the bed and fell asleep almost immediately.

Chapter 4

Again, it was her phone buzzing endlessly on the nightstand that woke Olivia up close to noontime. She had three missed calls from a Teamtastic colleague, an engineer who had also flown to Corfu to present a different project at the conference. Olivia was alarmed to see his name flashing on the screen. In a way, she had left him to face the crowd alone the day before.

With her heart beating fast against her ribcage and a glass of water to alleviate her mouth that suddenly became dry, Olivia called him back.

"Hey! Where are you?" he asked when he picked up the call.

"Hi, Lee. I'm in another … hotel. I'm sorry I …"

"I totally get it. I'm so sorry for what happened to you yesterday. I was worried about you. I didn't know where you were and called Doreen. She said she'd spoken to you but thought you were at the hotel, but I couldn't find you anywhere."

"I'm sorry. I just couldn't stay there."

Lee sighed. He was a nice guy who had begun working for the consultancy firm three years before. She had handled his hiring. "Listen, Olivia, I checked last night, just to … you know … Most of those who uploaded stuff to social media have private or anonymous accounts so we can't know who they were. I tried looking for names." This engineer sounded much more sympathetic than her direct *Human* Resources manager had been.

"Thanks, Lee. I didn't even think about that. I just want it all to go away. I booked a flight for tomorrow night. Doreen asked me to book the first one out."

"Okay. I hope it will turn out for the best. Usually, after the dust settles, everyone moves on to the next drama."

She noticed he spared her the details of how things looked now at the conference when the dust was still very much up in the air.

"Thank you, Lee. And thanks for understanding."

It was a wake-up call in more than one way.

Despite the inconceivably gorgeous blue and green view that peered from every window, all the heaviness of yesterday closed in on Olivia again. The colors outside were sharp and vivid under the June sun and wrapped in the fresh scent of an unpolluted area—so unlike the city she was calling home—yet her problems were still there, waiting for her. This little nest would have to be left behind and the ugly reality faced.

Her stomach gurgled, but she didn't feel hungry, which was strange.

"You're eating your issues," Daria had told her in what had been her last year with Jeff when she had strived to keep to the course of their relationship, to the path she had selected for herself.

"You have to get back on the market. Laser that thing off," Daria had said, pointing at Olivia's bikini line when Olivia had spent two weeks on Daria's couch, waiting to move into the smaller apartment that she had rented. "Buy some new clothes, or at least hang these at the front of your closet," Daria had added, spreading out a few sexier dresses and blouses, when she had helped Olivia settle into that apartment.

Daria Evans, the offspring of a realtor and a university professor, had been Olivia's guide to spinsterhood. While Olivia had spent ten years with one man, Daria had had four different long-term relationships and several Tinder flings.

"Maybe I love men too much to commit to just one. What will I do with all the rest?" she had said when they had sat on the couch in Daria's apartment, drinking white wine. Daria, with her wide, dark doe-eyes, lustrous black curls, and taut, curvy body was a marketing ninja, wooed by companies and men alike.

"I took a risk by breaking up with Jeff at almost thirty-eight, but better late than never, right?" Olivia had said, hugging one of Daria's velvet throw pillows.

"Are we talking biological clocks here?" Daria had asked. "If Jeff wasn't the one to bring the situation to a head by accepting that job, don't you think you'd be wasting even more time?"

Maybe Daria had been right. Maybe if Jeff hadn't taken that offer, they would still be meeting, exhausted in bed at night, with their laptops, until one of them fell asleep, with only a random date night where they mostly talked shop, and sex once a month or longer if one of them had been buried in a project.

Putting on the red summer dress that she had bought the day before, Olivia hoped that, while her relationship had died of natural causes, her career wouldn't die a violent one.

As she made her way through the cobbled village alleys, the breeze flapped the skirt of the dress against Olivia's thighs and the sun caressed her bare arms. Despite everything, the earthy tones of the houses' walls, the colorful wooden shutters, and the blazing bougainvilleas were uplifting. By the time she reached the taverna, she was looking forward to meeting Niko. He was a friendly face in this beautiful yet foreign place.

But Kostas and Elena were the only ones she saw moving between the bar, kitchen, and tables when she hesitated at the entrance.

Sitting again at the same window table, Olivia thought she discerned German from one of the next tables, despite the rather loud Greek music that played in the background. The three couples sitting there looked like tourists, but one of them held a lively chat with Elena while she served them. *Germans speaking Greek; not the kind that would wear "*I heart Greece*" shirts*, Olivia thought with a smile.

Kostas and Elena nodded at her in recognition, and she smiled back, wondering what they thought of her invasion into their non-touristic village and the not-for-rent house.

"*Kalimera*. Vegetarian?" Elena asked with a polite smile.

"Yes, thank you. *Efkharisto*," Olivia said, realizing she probably wouldn't get a menu and just eat whatever she would be served. Then, as Elena turned to go, Olivia added, "Is Niko here?"

"No, Niko, no," Elena said before continuing toward the kitchen.

Usually, when waiting alone, she would open her emails, Facebook, or Twitter, but in the last thirty-six hours, they had become her enemies. Instead, Olivia gazed through the window, her eyes following the few passersby. Across the street from her was what looked like an office and a little shop next to it. She wondered what people did here for work.

Elena placed a bowl of fresh salad with a large rectangle of feta cheese on top of it, and a plate with dolmades and other cooked stuffed vegetables. The mix of smells opened Olivia's appetite, which had died during her conversation with Lee.

When she placed her credit card on the table later, Elena took it. Going through her purse, Olivia extracted a twenty euros bill and placed it under her empty water glass. She hoped it would cover the tip that she hadn't left last night. But when Elena returned her card and saw the note, she pointed at it. "No, no, thank you."

Olivia smiled but left it there when she quit her seat.

On the sidewalk, Olivia screened her eyes with her arm as she looked at the balcony over the taverna, wondering if Niko was home. With nothing to do until her flight tomorrow evening, she felt anchorless. The hectic pace of her life back home didn't leave much room for thoughts and now she had too much time on her hands.

The loud grunt of an engine coming to a halt made her turn her head. The same bus that she had taken the day before now stopped on the other side of the street, a hundred feet to her right. Olivia crossed the street and jogged toward it.

Several stops later, on a sandy beach, holding her sandals in her hand, she watched through squinted eyes how everyone else were either inside the crystal water or lying on beach towels under the bright blue sky. With the smell of sunscreen mixing with that of salty water, her feet sinking in the warm, grainy sand, Olivia finally felt like a tourist on a Greek island.

The thought of remaining in her bra and panties and going into the enticing turquoise water nudged her, but Olivia knew she wouldn't dare. If Daria had been there, she could have persuaded her, and they would probably be splashing the cool water on each other by now. Alone, she continued strolling and enjoying the scenery, fully dressed.

With an ice cream cone in one hand, Olivia struggled to find her phone inside her bag when it rang an hour later. She searched for a place in the shade, feeling her shoulders burning red under the sun. When she finally managed to answer, Doreen's voice spoke into her ear.

She checked the time again. Three p.m. local time, which was six a.m. back home. Used to getting emails from her manager with time marks of six or even five a.m., she wasn't too surprised.

"You didn't tell me you weren't at the hotel and that you moved." No greeting preceded the accusation.

"I thought I mentioned it. I was confused yesterday. Sorry, I couldn't stay there."

"I understand. It must have been tough." A formal pause prefaced Doreen's next sentence. "I need you to hand your laptop over to Lee at the hotel."

Olivia, who was just licking melted ice cream from her finger, froze. "Why? I'm flying back tomorrow."

"I know, but I need you to leave it with him."

"Am I being fired?" The ice cream was now streaming freely down her fingers.

"We'll talk about what's next when you're back on Monday," Doreen said.

"If I'm being fired, just tell me. I know what handing over your computer immediately means." Olivia could practically hear her own bloodstream gushing in her ears. The ice cream she had swallowed threatened to make its way up her throat.

"I'm not firing you, but I need you to please hand your computer over to Lee."

"Doreen, do you realize that I'm the one who was publicly humiliated and that I did nothing to deserve this except being unaware that a computer reboot cancels the previous instant messenger settings?"

"I do. And you have my sympathy. We'll talk all about it next week. But, right now, I need you to—"

"Hand my computer over to Lee. Okay, I get it. I will. But if I'm fired, just tell me."

"Okay, thank you. I'll see you on Monday, Olivia," Doreen said, then hung up.

You'll see me never, a voice rang in Olivia's head.

She trudged to a nearby bin and threw the cone inside. Then, returning to the ice cream stand that she had bought it from, she took a few napkins and wiped her hands before continuing blankly to the bus stop that would take her back to the village, and the house, and her laptop.

The cicadas' song grated on Olivia's nerves as she made her way from the small village square, where the bus had dropped her off, to the house on the side of the hill. Having to go back to that hotel flipped her stomach, but Olivia bagged her laptop and walked out. The sun was high in the village sky, and the sea breeze carried a faint smell of lemons as she waited at the bus stop.

A poison-green convertible turned a corner from the alley behind the Teresi Taverna. It slowed down and stopped when it reached her. The passenger's side window was lowered.

"Oh, hi." Olivia's heart gave a little lurch as she bent to look inside.

"Need a ride somewhere?" Niko asked from the driver's seat, peering at her from over his sunglasses.

"Um, I don't know. I have to get to the Imperial Beach hotel, but that's on the other side of the island."

"Leaving us, are you?"

"Oh, no, I just have to drop something off there." Did he think she was running away without paying or saying thank you?

The smirk that spread on his face told her that he was just teasing her. "It's your lucky day. I'm going to Corfu Town for a meeting. I can drop you off there on the way."

"Really? That would be great!"

Niko leaned over the stick shift and opened the door for her from the inside.

"Thanks." She buckled up next to him.

With the sunglasses and a dark blue dress shirt over dark grey pants, he looked like a businessman on holiday. The interior of the car had that delicious smell that had emanated from him the evening before—freshness, water, the sea.

"Interesting color for a car," she quipped.

"The guy I bought it from must have been color blind."

"Yes, *he* must have been color blind." She laughed.

Niko returned her gaze and laughed, too. "Have you been to Corfu Town yet?" he asked. It was the capital of the island.

"No. I arrived at Corfu on Wednesday night and went straight to the hotel. Then, on Thursday morning, I … arrived here. So, I didn't see much of anything. But today, I went to Agios Georgios beach."

Niko looked at her for a moment before returning his gaze to the road ahead. "That's a beautiful, touristic beach. There are quieter ones, if you like those."

"I might have time to go to one more before I fly back home tomorrow evening." There was a strange twitch in her stomach.

"A very short stay. And not a very pleasant one." His intonation made it sound more like a question.

"That's not Corfu's fault." She chuckled dryly. "So, you're not working today?" She wanted to divert the conversation.

"Did some paperwork and now heading to a meeting at the bank."

Silence fell between them. Once or twice, she turned to look at him and met his gaze.

"Comfortable car," Olivia said after a while to dispel the quiet, facepalming herself internally for the strange choice of topic when there was such a lush green view outside to comment on. But it was better than asking him more about himself like she wanted to. She had gotten the impression yesterday that he wasn't too keen on talking about himself.

"Small, but you get used to it," he replied.

"You're used to bigger cars?" she asked, just to say something and because he gave her an opening.

Niko just smiled, his eyes glued to the windshield.

It's none of my business, she stopped herself from further asking questions.

He shifted into a lower gear as the car started descending the road, and the shores at the other side of the island seemed closer. Her eyes were drawn to the tan, strong palm that held the stick shift. There was more to him than he disclosed; she was almost certain.

"That's Corfu Town. We call it Kerkyra." He pointed toward a denser area.

"What's that hilly bulge over there?" Olivia pointed at what looked like a little mountain between the city and the sea.

"That's the old Venetian fort. You haven't watched James Bond?" Niko smirked.

"No. I don't watch those. Why? Was it shot there?"

"*For Your Eyes Only* was. Not just there. Anyway, your hotel is just a few kilometers after Corfu Town."

"After it?"

"Yes. But, by car, it will take just five minutes, so don't worry."

"Okay. Thanks, Niko."

"No problem." After another moment of silence, he added, looking at her, "When will you finish there?"

"Soon. I'm dropping off my laptop there. At a colleague's." Saying it out loud clogged her throat again.

Niko must have sensed the change in her voice because he turned to look at her.

Olivia chewed on her bottom lip. "I think I'm getting fired."

"I'm sorry," he said, moving his gaze between her and the road.

"That's okay. Thanks." She averted her gaze to the window to her right as tears now stung her eyes. It wasn't so much the job, the paycheck, or the prestige she had lost, though it was all of that, too. Everything she had worked for. Most of all, it was the humiliation and being deserted when she had done nothing wrong.

To busy herself, Olivia pulled her cell phone from her bag and texted Lee again, making sure he would meet her outside. She didn't want to go inside.

A text from Daria was waiting for her. "*How are you today? Can't wait to see you soon. I hope you're better and that things are settling down.*"

Looking at Niko, she caught him side-eyeing her. She ran a hand over her hair. She felt frumpy despite the nice red dress and sandals that she had on.

"Who's Thalia?" she heard herself asking, and she couldn't believe the question that had just escaped her lips. It came out of nowhere, out of a free association that was playing in her mind. What was happening to her? She could usually keep her impulses in check.

Niko seemed to be just as baffled, snapping his head toward her. "A friend," he said, returning his gaze to the windshield.

"I'm sorry, it's none of my business. I was wondering who Elena was, too. I know Kostas is your uncle." She futilely hoped her pathetic attempt had saved the situation.

"Elena is Kostas' wife. She came from the mainland."

"The mainland?" Olivia was happy at the opportunity to divert the conversation yet again.

"From Thessaloniki. The mainland is the part of Greece that isn't the islands."

They were now fast approaching the hotel and the area looked familiar. As much as she didn't feel like seeing it or anyone there, she was happy to soon leave the car. For some reason, her mouth blurted stupid things next to Niko. He was good-looking and nice, and something about him interested her, but he was just a guy working in a taverna in a remote village on the other side of the world and they had zero in common.

Out here, alone, with everything she had built and clung to for years tumbling down and crumbling like sand between her fingers, she was in a state to think that his life, which was as far as possible from her own, was enticing. Or maybe it was just calmer and less stressful than hers had been.

Without another exchange between them, Niko drove up the driveway and stopped the car at the front of the large hotel.

They both turned to look at each other.

Olivia pressed her lips together. "Thank you," she said, and it came out as a half-whisper.

"If you want to wait, I can be here in about forty-five minutes and drive you back," he said.

She bit the inside of her lip. She would have to hide somewhere until he returned.

"Okay, thanks," she said and unbuckled.

Standing at the foot of the stairs that led to the entrance, Olivia smiled at Niko as he drove off, then pressed the call button on her phone. "I'm outside," she said.

Chapter 5

Lee descended the marble steps five minutes later, wearing a nametag with the conference logo.

Olivia got up from the low stone wall she had been waiting on. "Hi."

"Hey, Olivia. Doreen dragged me into this. I'm sorry."

"That's okay; don't worry about it." She opened her backpack and pulled out her laptop. "Here." She handed it to him then clasped her hands together.

"Is there anything I can do to help?" he asked, shifting slightly on his feet.

She let out a huffed chuckle. "No, thank you, Lee. You've been kinder than … I appreciate it." She didn't want to name her manager, though it was obvious.

After he left, she went back to sit on the stone wall that stretched along a flowerbed from the entrance of the hotel almost to the end of the driveway. She sat as far from the entrance as possible, wondering if she should hide somewhere until Niko's return.

With her face buried in her cell phone screen, Olivia didn't notice the man who was coming toward her until he stood right before her.

"Hey, Olivia. How are you?"

"Emmet! Hi!"

"Leaving already?" he asked.

"Um, yes."

"I saw Lee …" he explained. "I'm sorry for what happened there yesterday. I wish you'd stay."

She didn't reply. On his nametag, next to his name, appeared the name of the company he represented, TechCell. In the aftermath, Olivia had managed to forget the part about "*the cute guy from TechCell*" in the infamous message.

"Listen, Olivia, since I'm the only one from TechCell here, can I assume …?" He must have caught her staring at his nametag.

Oh no. She covered her face with her palms. "I'm sorry about that. Please, just ignore it. I'm sorry if it made you feel uncomfortable." Didn't Greece have volcanos? She hoped it did and that one would erupt at that moment and spare her this additional humiliation.

"No, no, I was flattered. Everyone came to me after and …"

Olivia removed her hands from her face and stared at him as he continued to describe how her most humiliating moment had made him popular. He even hinted he could rectify the issues that Daria had mentioned in her private message to her. At some point, the words stopped making sense, as if she was hearing them from a distance. His lips continued moving and, slowly, the words became discernible again.

"If you want, you know, I still have a room here. Hey, I think you're cute, too. I have a girlfriend, but what happens in Greece stays in Greece, right?" He grinned at her and winked.

She wanted to throw up. How could she ever think this man was attractive?

He then placed his hand on her shoulder and rubbed it.

"Take your hand off me," she hissed, jerking her shoulder so his hand fell off.

"Relax, I was just …"

A car pulled up next to them.

"Olivia, I'm here." Niko was standing just outside the open driver's door, leaning his arm on the car's roof, his sunglasses on top of his head, and his eyes intent on Emmet, who took a step back.

Olivia inhaled sharply then exhaled evenly to slow down her racing heart. "Hi," she said, and it came out a bit shaky.

Niko slammed the car's door and took a step forward. "Need help with that bag?" He jutted his chin toward her.

Her bag wasn't big, and his clear hint was well taken by Emmet who muttered, "Bye, Olivia," and scuttled away.

Swallowing, she shouldered her bag and went to the car. "Thanks."

"Everything okay?" He was still standing outside, at the other side of the car from her. "I saw that he …"

"Yes, everything's fine," she hurried to say. Her heart was in her throat.

They climbed into the car and Niko turned to look at her. "Are you sure you're okay?"

She just nodded, feeling his gaze lingering on her profile before he pulled away.

"Do you want to see Corfu Town before you leave?" he asked after a moment's silence.

She looked at him. "Sure." It came out less certain than she had intended it to sound.

"We can just drive by."

"No, I'd like to see it. I could use the diversion," she said with a faint smile.

Niko pressed his lips together and nodded once.

In a few minutes, they parked at the foot of the large fortress she had seen from a distance, at the Spianáda square, which Niko explained was the largest square in Greece. From there, they walked into the pedestrians-only area behind it, a beautiful mix of Venetian and Mediterranean architecture, terra cotta rooftops and wrought-iron balconies, overflowing flowerpots, as well as majestic-looking buildings and monuments. Niko pointed and explained about the most prominent ones.

"Now you finally feel like you're in Europe, right?" he asked, smiling.

She returned his gaze. "From day one. But yes, this does look like a classic old European city. I've always wanted to visit."

They passed by boutiques, tavernas, souvenir shops, a normal-sized pharmacy where she could probably find her brand of contacts, art galleries, a hair dresser. Olivia sent a well-practiced hand to inspect the volume her curls had reached in the humid Greek afternoon. She memorized the location of the hair salon. It was an automatic habit whenever she traveled; so automatic that it didn't occur to her that she was leaving the next evening. She reached into her pocket, extracted a simple scrunchie, then tied her hair up in a tight bun.

"We can get a good vegetarian dinner here and filtered American coffee," Niko said with that lopsided smile, pointing at a cozy-looking taverna.

Olivia smirked back. "I'm more of an espresso kind of gal."

It wasn't one of the overly touristic establishments that they had passed by, that imitated Parisian coffee shops, with side-by-side chairs outside, where customers could sit and people-gaze.

They went in, and Niko led the way to a window table. A menu in Greek and English was brought the minute they sat down.

"They still like tourists here," she teased, eliciting a smirk on Niko's face.

They ordered a vegetarian platter for her and a souflaki for him, with two glasses of wine.

"I don't want to pry, just to make sure that you're okay," Niko said after the waiter left. "That guy at the hotel?"

"Yes, thank you, I'm fine. He's just another … *malaka*. I've seen too many of these recently. So, tell me, when you sit in other tavernas, are you comparing them to yours?"

Niko nodded before he spoke, as if acknowledging the first part of her reply before answering her obvious avoidant question. "Of course I'm benchmarking and analyzing; value chain, pain points, actionable items."

Olivia chided herself internally for not expecting this business terminology from him. "You're well-versed in marketing lingo. So, why don't you like tourists in Aleniki?"

Niko took a visible deep breath before replying, "To make Aleniki touristic, we would need to submit it to significant development that would change the essence of it. This can only bring income for a few months every year, but what happens in the off-season? Then there are the foreigners who want to buy properties, and some of us received offers, but that would also change the essence of the place and raise the cost of living and housing for everyone. So, no one's interested in this. At least, not so far. We see what happens in other places, where a population of five hundred drowns in a population of three thousand during the summer. We're just two hundred, and we're good with our little spot staying as it is."

She found herself staring at him.

Niko shrugged. "Besides, we want to dance when we feel like it, not because tourists expect a *Zorba, The Greek* folklore show with their dinner."

Olivia was surprised into a laugh. "You should have said *that* yesterday right when I walked in." She then took a sip of wine, hoping he would be willing to answer her next question. "Yesterday, you said something about *coming back*. You didn't always live there?"

"No."

"Cryptic," she dared to push it.

"Not cryptic. I spent years away from Greece."

"Abroad? What did you do?"

Niko seemed to ponder his reply. "I was a financial attaché in the Greek embassy in several countries. The last one was the Netherlands."

Olivia was glad she wasn't sipping her wine at that moment, or she would be choking right now. Of all the things she had imagined he did, being a diplomat hadn't been one of them. He seemed so laid-back, local, direct, so *undiplomatic* that she couldn't even fathom.

Her face must have revealed her thoughts because Niko then added, smiling, "Surprised?"

"Well … yes." She smiled. "I have, like, a million questions."

"It's not so complicated." Niko took a sip of wine.

"Why did you return?"

"I realized I wasn't in the right place for me."

"Your family must have been thrilled that you came back."

A muscle twitched in his jaw. "That's a bit more complicated."

She took the hint. "So, what does a financial attaché do?" The question had her imagining Niko in a business suit and tie. Given that he looked so good in his bank-meeting clothes, it wasn't too hard to imagine how good he would look in formal wear.

"Kind of what you'd expect from the name of it."

He was so unlike Jeff, who could pass an entire evening with friends at a restaurant talking about his software engineering projects.

"How did you get to working in embassies?"

"I studied Finance. My father encouraged me. He thought it'd be good for the family business or the island." His expression and tone seemed to convey a sort of sadness over his father's humble aspirations. "When I finished, I took the tests for civil service and was offered a job in the Foreign Ministry. I accepted it. After a few years, I was offered to serve abroad."

"You probably nailed it on those tests. Your father must have been even prouder of you. How long did you do it for?"

"Fifteen years. And my father is dead," he said, and an almost visible cloud crossed his face. He didn't explain, and it was obvious he wasn't going to.

Before she had a chance to respond, he added, "What about you? You came here for a conference, right? But, what about? What do *you* do?"

"I'm a Human Resources consultant. I came here to present a project." Olivia realized that he couldn't know everything from overhearing her conversation with Daria. "An embarrassing personal message from my best friend jumped up on the screen right before my speech. People filmed it and uploaded it to social media with my name and all. I ran away."

"Shit. I'm sorry," he said. "I'm sorry that happened to you. It explains a lot." He leaned forward, his hand hovering over hers before he pulled it back.

The sincerity in his honey-green eyes and Niko's tone of voice made tears sting the back of Olivia's throat again. Describing it out loud for the first time was hard, but he and Lee were being her friends where she had none.

Olivia quenched the urge to show him one of the posts. She had a strong feeling that Niko would be a

Lee and not an Emmet about it. But the part about getting under a hot Greek guy to rectify her lifeless sex life stopped her.

She sighed. "I told you I met too many *malaka*s recently."

"That guy at the hotel?"

"Yes, he's one."

"And you think you'll get fired because of it?"

She breathed in. "I don't know. I think so. It sounded like it."

"What was your presentation about?"

She swooned inside. She wasn't sure why. Maybe because he didn't pry into the raunchy details. And it was as if his question was an act of kindness. She never got to present.

"It's a summary of a two-year project. I worked with one of my clients on creating programs and organizational changes that increased their employees' productivity and innovation. We also tackled employee relations issues and crisis management." She scoffed. "I consult others about handling crises."

"A personal crisis is different."

"I have no idea how to handle it, though I know what I'd consult my manager." She sighed.

"You'll find a way. Sometimes, the only way to face a storm is to let it pass over you. When things become clearer, you can start cleaning the mess."

"You're a crisis counselor, too?" she joked, but he seemed to know firsthand what he was talking about.

"People take consultants to tell them what they already know, but they prefer believing someone else rather than themselves."

"Ouch."

"You know I'm right." He smiled that candid, charming smile of his.

"Usually, I'd give you an entire lecture about why you're wrong. But, A, I'm too tired, and B, I don't know what's right anymore." She didn't mention the third reason—that she sensed he understood more about this world and human nature than she, the Human Resources consultant, did.

"Deep down, you know. Trust yourself." His eyes were intent on her and his gaze caressing. Then, as if he sensed she needed it, he added in a lighter tone, "You know what's good for all occasions, good or bad? Rakomelo."

She laughed, happy to have the mood uplifted, and he ordered her another glass.

"You're not having one?"

"I'm driving."

Soon, they were in the car again and on their way back to the village. A comforting mist inside her head took the edge off the day's murk. The last two hours that she had spent in Niko's company had helped. Except for a few words and gazes they exchanged, the music that played on the car radio and the steady hum of the engine were the only sounds.

The silence was broken again when they approached Aleniki.

"When's your flight?" Niko asked.

"Tomorrow evening."

He parked in an alley behind the taverna. "I'll walk you to the house."

"I can walk there; that's okay. Thanks for the lift to the hotel and back. And for dinner."

He didn't reply but just continued beside her. As they turned the corner of the alley and onto the main street, the lights from his taverna were seen spilling onto the sidewalk. She thought he would turn left and go there, but he continued next to her, crossing the street and then into the smaller alleys behind it.

"It's not dangerous here at night, right?" she asked.

"No."

Something in the pit of her stomach felt familiar and strange. Something she hadn't felt in a long time. It was the opposite of how her stomach had felt when Emmet had spoken to her.

Olivia ran a hand over her hair. Little strands were coming loose, curling around her face. Her palms tingled with a mix of nervousness and excitement.

As they reached the small house, Niko stopped at the foot of the veranda. "Goodnight, Olivia," he said, then turned to leave.

She just stood there, a bit stumped. She had been sure he had walked her here for a reason. Not that something was bound to have happened, but she liked the thought of that reason.

"Niko," she called after his retreating back.

He turned around.

"Thanks," she just said.

"You're welcome." He then turned to leave again.

"Do you want to …? Do you want to come in?" It must have been the two glasses of wine that she had consumed, mixed with the disintegration of everything she had been used to, as well as his good looks and kind treatment of her that pushed her to do something she hadn't done in over a decade, or never, really.

Niko spun around yet again and looked at her.

Olivia shrugged. She couldn't undo the words now.

Instead of answering, he closed the distance between them and locked his eyes on hers. The look in them, and his tone of voice, communicated that he fully comprehended. "It could have been great, but you had a long day and have a flight tomorrow." He placed his hands on her biceps and added, "I'll see you tomorrow, Olivia." With a soft, half-smile, he left.

It could have been an embarrassing moment of rejection, but it wasn't. With his palms sending warm waves down her body, and the sincerity in his expression and voice, Niko had let her understand that he knew she hadn't really meant it and had attributed it to her circumstances. He was considerate enough to not take advantage of it, on the one hand; and to not make her feel rejected, on the other hand.

Chapter 6

To kill time and evaporate the wine and that rollercoaster of a day, Olivia showered, then packed all her belongings into her backpack and the clothing shop's tote. Going over the rooms to make sure she hadn't forgotten anything, she explored the little house that belonged to Niko's family as if for the first time. She took in the vintage furniture, the calm, light blue and cream colors, the few paintings and old pictures of Corfu that hung on the walls. The large painting above the fireplace in the living room was especially beautiful. Moving closer to admire the beach painted in it, the painter's signature caught her eyes. *Thalia.*

Olivia returned to look at the other paintings. Two of them had Thalia's signature. She remembered Niko had mentioned she had helped him decorate. Did he mean with the paintings? Was she an artist? An ex-girlfriend? Or both?

Either way, it was none of her business. Still, it made her even more self-conscious about her blatant offer to him earlier. Good thing she was leaving the next day. This island had brought nothing but unpredicted events and atypical behavior from her.

~~~~~~~~~~~~~~~~~~~~~~~~~~~~~~~

Being her last day, Olivia managed to push back the awkwardness over meeting Niko again. At first, she only wanted to see him so she could thank him and insist on paying for the house and meals. However, after leaving money and a "thank you" note on the kitchen counter, she realized she just wanted to see him one last time. She had no excuse as to why.

As she walked into the taverna at noon, dressed in her new jeans and an olive green blouse, only Elena was there to smile warmly at her.

Sitting at the table that she secretly referred to as hers, Olivia looked around but didn't see him anywhere. There were just a few other occupied tables. A few of the faces had become familiar.

In a moment, Elena arrived with a tray that contained the delicacies that Olivia liked and a few that were new to her.

"*Efkharisto poly*, Elena," Olivia said, proud to use the additional "very much" to her thank you.

She later tucked a twenty euros bill under the tray for the reluctant Elena.

Just as she was ready to leave, thinking that it was actually good that Niko wasn't there, because it was only her being out of her element that wanted to see him, he entered through a back door behind the bar.

He spotted her and motioned her with his hand to wait. Arriving at her table with two cups of coffee, he put one in front of her and sat down across the round table from her.

"Thanks," she said, running a hand over her hair and trying to ignore the fact that her heart skipped a beat at the sight of him.

"When do you leave for the airport?" he asked, then took a sip of coffee.

"I have to be there at five, so I thought to leave here at four."

"I'll drive you," he said. He might have noticed her mouth opening to reject his offer because he then added, "I already asked Kostas to cover for me here. I'll drive you."

"Niko," she started but didn't know what to add. In her two days here, except for the ouzo and pretending-to-not-know-English incident, he had been nothing but kind and generous toward her. She wanted to say something more than the "thank you" that eventually left her lips.

"Don't mention it."

A man peered into the bar from the back door that had been left open and called Niko's name.

"Excuse me," he said. "We have a lot of arrangements today. There's a wedding tomorrow, and they're holding the reception here. I'll see you at four." He then disappeared through the door behind the bar.

If she took a taxi to the airport, as she had planned, this could have been the last she had seen of Niko, Olivia thought as she made her way through the village alleys back to the house. Instead, she would get to spend more time with him on the ride there. She endeavored to ignore the emotional seesaw that had her wavering between wanting to see him, to hoping to evade him, to being happy to spend time with him. She also shunned the fact that she would never see him again after today.

With two and a half hours to kill, she found supplies in a utility closet and cleaned the house, aiming to leave it as she had found it. It was small enough for her to finish it all and take a quick shower after. Changing the sheets on the bed, she thought of Niko again. This had been his bed and, although she was alone, Olivia felt her face flaming up. Last night, she had pretty much offered him to get into it with her.

On the veranda, thinking she should catch up before Monday to see if any new disaster had befallen while she had hidden herself away from the world, Olivia opened the Teamtastic Outlook account on her phone. She skimmed over the subject lines and the senders' names. One email invited her to a briefing on DoITmore so that a colleague could take the account over from her. While it wasn't surprising, it still hurt. Another was a company-wide email sent from the CEO of Teamtastic. "*How we deal with the current situation*," the title read.

Reading the content, black spots started dancing in front of Olivia's eyes. Her CEO announced, company-wide, that the threats of DoITmore and TechCell to sue were intercepted, that no legal actions were taking place; and that, while TechCell had decided to cancel their contract, DoITmore would continue their business with the agency. She also instructed everyone not to speak to the press, address the issue on social media, or discuss it with clients and competitors.

Placing the cell phone face down on the patio table and flumping onto the ornamented chair,

Olivia buried her face in her hands. She had become a liability, a PR issue. Going into the office on Monday would be a walk of shame. A company-wide email had been the final nail in the coffin of her ability to somehow survive this with dignity.

Anger bubbled inside her. This could have been a storm in a teacup if people hadn't purposefully magnified it. Who knew what discount DoITmore managed to milk out of her CEO?

One thing had become clear—she wouldn't go back there on Monday just to be further humiliated. She wouldn't go back there, period.

It was a quarter to seven a.m. in Seattle when Olivia dialed Doreen's number, pacing the veranda from side to side, her palms tingling and sweating.

"I just saw Marlene's email," she managed to say, though her throat felt like the Sahara. "Doreen, I know you're going to fire me, so why don't you save us both the inconvenience?"

"Listen, Olivia …"

Olivia sighed. "Just be honest with me. Please."

There was dead silence on the other side of the line.

"Are you there?"

"Yes, Olivia … I'm …" Doreen faltered, then stopped.

"You know what? I quit." It came out as a dejected acquiescence rather than a bold declaration. When no reply came, Olivia hung up, feeling the pulse beating in her temples.

Two minutes later, while she was pacing the veranda numbly, a text message pinged on her phone. "*Check your email,*" the message read. "*I was going to give you this on Monday. I'm sorry. D.*" Another ping brought in another message. "*I'll ignore our recent conversation so you'll get severance pay.*"

The email contained a termination letter.

The magnificent view in front of her blurred as Olivia sat on the patio chair and took her glasses off.

This was not how things were supposed to happen. This was not how she saw herself at the age of thirty-eight. She was supposed to be rocking a vibrant career that would justify all her honorary accolades, be married to a successful man, having at least one kid, and managing it all without breaking a sweat more than once a week. Her modified plans included a civil ceremony or notary agreement signing with Jeff sometime when their schedules would enable it, working on a pregnancy soon after, and getting more high-profile projects at work, followed by a promotion.

How did things get from *that* to *this*?

Just the thought of her empty apartment in Seattle, where she would have to spend days looking for a job, then interviewing in an industry where everyone knew everything, and going out on dates in parallel, made her want to throw up into the nearest flower pot.

"I can't do this," she mumbled into her palms.

"Olivia." A voice coming from the side of the house startled her.

She rubbed her palms over her face and put her glasses back on.

"Olivia?" Niko showed up from the narrow path that encircled the house.

"Hi," she said, rising to her feet.

"Hi. I was … I knocked on the front door, but you didn't answer. Are you ready? Is everything okay?"

"It's four," she said, suddenly realizing the time. "Sorry. I didn't notice. I was fired. I quit, but I was fired, too." Her chest tightened. "It's a mess. A public mess."

Niko climbed the three steps that separated the veranda from the sloping stretch of grass and the grove beyond it. "I'm really sorry," he said, searching and holding her gaze.

"Thanks."

"Is there anything I can do?"

She inhaled. "Niko, how much would renting this house for a longer period cost?" It came right out, as if it had been on the tip of her tongue all along.

He tilted his head, watching her through narrowed eyes. "Why?"

She breathed out slowly. "I don't want to go back there just yet. Maybe I just need a few more days, a week, I don't know. Until I'm ready, which I'm not at the moment." She felt she was rambling.

"I don't know what the prices on the market are." It was an obvious evasion.

She hadn't thought of it when she had blurted it out, but now Olivia was worried that she had imposed on him, or worse, that he would think she wanted to stay because of him, because of last night.

"Fair enough. You know what? I miss being in a city and Corfu Town—"

"You're welcome to stay here, Olivia," he cut her off. "It's not that. Just don't ask me to name a price. I'm not looking to make money off this place." He had a way of letting her know he clocked her meaning without throwing it in her face.

"I can't stay here for free. Maybe I could help with something? With the taverna?"

He averted his gaze for a moment before returning it to her. "I'm not doing this so you'll feel obligated. The place would be closed up, anyway, if you weren't here."

"I'll be happy to help. Anything you need."

"It's not an office job, Olivia," he challenged with a tilt of his head.

Olivia's eyes were involuntarily drawn to his T-shirt-clad wide shoulders that seemed the result of physical work. "I know. I waited on tables back in the day." She didn't add that it had been for a week during her first year in university before her father arranged an internship for her in his friend's firm.

"Are you sure you know what you're doing? Just staying here?" he reality-checked her.

She breathed out. "No, I don't. But I know that, right now, I prefer … not going back."

"Hiding. Wouldn't people worry about you? Your family? Friends?"

"Originally, I was supposed to stay for a few days of vacation after the conference ended, but that's … that got canceled, so you could say that I'm just going with my old plan." She shrugged. A six months old plan for a Greek island getaway she had made with Jeff. His lack of enthusiasm should have been an indication of what had followed.

"Okay. We could use more working hands at the wedding, if you're up for it."

"I am!"

"Okay. Come over later, and I'll show you around."

"Great. Thank you, Niko." She wanted to hug him but raised a thumbs-up, instead.

Niko wrapped his palm around her thumb and fist. "Be careful doing this with older people here. This gesture is considered offensive in Greece."

"Oh, wow," she muttered, acutely aware of the warmth of his hand wrapped around hers. "Why is it offensive?"

"For people above fifty, this would be the equivalent of giving someone the middle finger anywhere else."

"Thanks for letting me know, or I'd thumb everyone up." Her hand was still in his.

"I'll see you later." Niko removed his hand and smiled.

Unpacking later and washing panties and a bra under the bathroom sink so she would have enough clothes for a few more days, the full enormity of what she was doing by staying had accosted Olivia.

It was so unlike her. Then again, the entire situation that she had found herself in was unlike her.

She texted a casual throw-them-off-the-scent text to the three people in her life. "*Don't laugh, but I decided to stay for a few days' vacation. Doreen knows.*" She purposefully didn't delve into the recent development because, right now, their concern, plethora of advice, and immediate call to action would be too much. Her father would start sending her links to job sites, and her mother would say things like, "I talked to Maria Soltis. Her son works in Microsoft. He'll be on the lookout for you. And, by the way, he's divorced and they only have one kid."

A reply came in from Daria not long after. "*Good girl! Now use Tinder for fuck's sake. That's exactly why I installed it for you. Pun intended.*"

Olivia chuckled. Daria knew she had disabled the app after one coffee-date only, one that had lasted forty minutes before the guy pocketed the tip that she had left for the waitress.

~~~~~~~~~~~~~~~~~~~~~~~~~~~~~~~~

Before going to the taverna, Olivia stopped by the local grocery store and bought things she could use to make simple meals with, then took them back to the house before returning to the main street.

Several tables outside the taverna were full. She nodded to a few familiar faces. Inside, the place was arranged differently than usual—tables were clustered together to create larger seating area, and those along the window were lined up and looked ready to accommodate the bridal party.

An orchestra of voices speaking, and crockery and silverware clanking against a metal surface was heard from the kitchen.

"Hello," Olivia called, hesitating to just walk in. "*Kalispera.*"

Niko's head appeared in the kitchen door. "Hi, come on in; meet everyone." He then looked back into the kitchen and said something in Greek.

Olivia followed him inside.

The industrial kitchen was about the size of the main living space in the house that he let her stay in. Elena and a younger woman were busy arranging sets of blue and white ornated ceramic dishes, while Kostas unloaded the contents of heavy boxes and crates into various shelves and a large industrial refrigerator.

"Olivia, you know Elena and Kostas. This is their daughter, my cousin, Ioannina. We call her Nina."

They all greeted her; Kostas with a half-smile and a nod, Elena with a strong accent, "Hello, Olivia," and Nina with a smiling, "Nice to meet you. Welcome!"

Olivia greeted them back, sending a smile to each. "How can I help?"

Niko, resuming his work with Kostas, said, "Nina and you will arrange things outside. She'll show you everything."

Nina flicked her long, heavy-looking braid of brown hair from her shoulder to her back and grabbed one of the piles of dishes. "Olivia, if you can take another pile, we'll put them on the bar. From there, we'll arrange them on the tables after we finish with decorating."

Two hours saw Olivia and Nina dressing tables and chairs with matching fabrics that they had brought from the storage. Olivia got to be behind the bar and exit through the back door to the storage room and the open space at the back of the building through which she could see Niko's green car parked in the alley behind it. Dishes, silverware, and wine glasses were placed, and colorful glass pebbles were scattered artfully on the tables.

Time flew by. She hardly exchanged a word with anyone but Nina. Once, Niko, who was carrying boxes of bottles that were brought by a delivery van, asked if she was okay. Her eyes were unconsciously drawn to the visible flexing muscles of his arms just where his black T-shirt's short sleeves ended.

A girl, who looked twenty, served the customers outside.

"That's another relative, Althea. She works here sometimes," Nina explained.

Kostas moved his bulky figure between the kitchen and the bar, and a woman who looked just like Elena, only older and with her hair naturally silver, joined Elena in the kitchen.

"That's my aunt, Anastasia," Nina explained. "She and my mother will cook."

"Now they start cooking for tomorrow?"

"No, they've been working on it for two days, but now they're preparing the things that have to be fresh. Some of it will be done tomorrow morning. They're trained in this. It's not the first celebration we have here."

"Is it only people from the village who rent the place for celebrations or …?"

"No, from all over. People like that it's not touristic. And besides, my mom's and my aunt's cooking is famous."

When, according to Nina, they had finished most of the work, there was leisure to talk. Sitting at a table and folding napkins, Olivia learned that Nina was younger than Niko, who turned out to be thirty-nine, not far from what she had estimated him to be. She lived in the village with her husband and two kids and was a kindergarten teacher in a larger village. Her father, Kostas, was Niko's late father's younger brother. Nina was talkative and spoke English well.

"I worked in hotels here until I had my first son." She spoke freely of her work, family, and shared pictures of her two sons.

When Nina attempted to pry into her circumstances—"Niko just said you came to stay and liked Corfu and wanted to stay a bit more"—a woman entered the taverna from the street, calling cheerfully in Greek.

Just as Olivia turned her head to look at the newcomer, Niko entered through the door behind the bar. "Thalia," he called, adding a few short sentences in Greek. As the two met just across the floor from where Olivia and Nina sat, they kissed each other on both cheeks.

A twinge of jealousy darted in Olivia's stomach. This time, it wasn't a random *I wish I had a friend here, too* kind of pinch, as she had experienced on her first night, but specific to seeing a woman close to Niko. It shouldn't have surprised her, but it did.

She lowered her head, back to focusing on the napkin that she was folding.

"Olivia, hi. Nina, *ya*," Thalia greeted each in a different language from across the room. Olivia had learned that "ya" was the familiar shorthand for "*Yassas*," or hello.

In a silk, beige jumpsuit that not every woman could wear as casually beautiful as Thalia was wearing it, and with her shiny brown hair that would never look like parsley avalanching down her shoulders, she approached them with a radiant smile.

Niko disappeared into the kitchen that now produced mouthwatering scents.

Olivia and Nina smiled back, and Nina said something in Greek, rising to her feet to exchange kisses on both cheeks with Thalia.

"I heard you stayed and that you're helping at the wedding reception," Thalia said, looking at Olivia. "You'll love it! Forget about the touristic tavernas you probably saw. Tomorrow, you will see the real thing." She seemed cheerful at the prospect.

"I'm looking forward to it," Olivia replied. "I haven't been to the touristic tavernas, so I'm glad I'll get the real deal right from the start."

"Will you be here?" Nina asked Thalia in English.

"No, I'm leaving to Mykonos for a few days, to run a yoga and art workshop."

Of course you are, a voice cut through Olivia's thoughts. She strove to shush it. It had no place to form.

"So, you're an artist?" she asked, instead. "I saw a few of your paintings in the house I …" She wanted to say *I rent*, but, since Niko didn't let her pay, she couldn't find a better term.

"Yes, these are mine. I teach art."

"Teach art!" Nina scoffed. "She's an art professor and a yoga instructor," she corrected proudly, looking at Olivia.

"Not professor," Thalia remarked.

"Yet!" Nina enthused.

Olivia resolved to chat Nina later into revealing Thalia's connection to them. To Niko.

When children's squeals were heard coming from the street, Nina rose to her feet. "That's my husband coming to pick me up."

Two young boys ran into the taverna and threw their arms around their mother's hips. She bent and kissed their heads, mumbling to them in Greek.

Thalia and Olivia watched the three.

"He's outside in the car. I'll see you tomorrow, Olivia," Nina said, then added a sentence in Greek to Thalia while grabbing her purse and kissing Thalia again on both cheeks.

"I'd better go, too," Thalia said when it was just her and Olivia. "I only came to say goodbye and leave Niko my keys."

Olivia didn't know what to say, so she just smiled and nodded, feeling silly.

"Enjoy tomorrow," Thalia said and turned to leave.

"Have a safe travel."

I should probably get going, too, Olivia thought, arranging the napkins on a nearby table.

The kitchen door was opened and a surge of wonderful scents filled the space. Niko came through it, carrying a transparent plastic bag that contained a few plastic boxes.

"This is from Elena," he said, handing it to her. "All vegetarian."

She gasped. "That's so sweet of her! I bought things at the grocery today, but nothing will taste like this, I'm sure."

"Was everything okay? You're sure you're not regretting it?"

"Not at all. Thanks for letting me help. It was fun. Nina is sweet, and it was good doing something." She looked around at the decorated space. "And the place looks so different."

Niko brushed his gaze over his taverna. "Yes, it does," he said, sounding somewhat pensive. Olivia took the opportunity to skim her eyes over his face now that she knew his age. She felt an urge to trace her finger on the crease lines on his forehead and at the sides of his eyes and mouth.

"Well, I should go," she blurted, surprised yet again by the sensations he arose in her. "Unless there's something else you need me to do tonight," she added, blushing while she spoke, as the words wore a different shape in her head while she had said them.

"No, everything is pretty much ready. Thanks for helping. You didn't have to do it."

"I wanted to. I'm not used to not working. When should I be here tomorrow?"

"Ten would be good," he said.

"Should I wear anything special, or do you have a uniform?"

"No, freestyle," he replied, smiling. "Just something comfortable."

"Sounds good." She hesitated, wanting to hang around more in his company but not trusting herself. "Goodnight, Niko." She wondered when Greeks considered two people to be familiar enough with each other to kiss on both cheeks.

"Goodnight," he echoed.

She was ultra aware of his hand hovering close to the small of her back as he escorted her to the entrance.

Forking the dolmades at the kitchen counter later, Olivia thought that, so far, Niko easily checked more boxes on the list of what she could want in a man than most men she had met. He also made her feel things that she hadn't felt in a long while.

Too bad she was only a visitor. Too bad he didn't seem interested in her. Too bad she didn't know what the deal with Thalia was.

Chapter 7

While getting ready the next morning, Olivia called her mother. The green and blue view that smiled at her from every window of the cozy house helped her cope with lying by omission.

"I haven't been on a vacation since Christmas, so I'm taking it now." She hated lying, but it had to be done. She didn't want to worry her parents and have their onerous concern guiding her every action.

When that was done, she was ready. Her hair was pulled back into a tight bun. It had been on the tip of her tongue the night before to ask Nina if she had a blow dryer she could borrow, but she had been too shy at the last minute to ask. In a pair of fitted jeans and a black V-neck soft blouse, along with her black canvas sneakers, the ones she had on for the long flight to Greece, she thought she looked fit to be considered a part of the taverna staff.

On the veranda, she called Daria.

"No, I didn't open Tinder, and I'm not going to," she said, laughing, as soon as Daria picked up.

"Baby steps, that's fine," Daria piped. Olivia could almost hear her smirk.

She then told her the truth.

"Oh no! I'm so sorry, sweetie! That bitch, Doreen, and that bigger bitch, Marlene. They don't deserve you if they couldn't have your back on this. I can get you an interview with one of my clients. I'm positive you could land something better."

"Thank you, sweets, but I don't want to think about it right now." Olivia's eyes were glued to the sea view. She couldn't fathom at that moment being stranded again under fluorescent lights for days on end.

"Don't thank me. It's the least I can do after my goddamn text got you into so much trouble. I keep going back to that. I wish I could undo it. But, hey, don't think about this now. Go get your pale self under some Greek sun and some Greek guy, you hear me?"

Olivia laughed. "I'll do my best. In the meantime, I'm helping here in a local taverna in exchange for free board."

"Why do I have a feeling that there's more to it than you're telling me?"

"I wish there was."

A male voice was heard in the background on Daria's end of the line.

"You have company?" Olivia asked.

"Just Tyler," Daria said, not even concerned that her friend-with-benefits would hear her referring to him like that.

"Tell him I said hi." Olivia wished she could be a bit more like Daria.

~~~~~~~~~~~~~~~~~~~~~~~~~~~~~~~~~~~~~

Maybe it was her improved mood, or maybe it was the nicely-dressed passersby on her way to the taverna, but Olivia could taste Sunday in the fresh air. The sun was bright and warm, but the sea and mountain breeze freshened it all up.

The tables outside the taverna were already decorated with flower arrangements. From the entrance, the place looked even more ready than it had been the evening before. Greek music played in the empty space and, even over it, she could hear the commotion from the kitchen that emanated intense smells.

Niko and a much-younger man entered the bar from the back.

Olivia's breath shallowed at the sight of Niko in a black dress shirt folded to his elbows and a dark olive-green tie. She stopped at the bar and, from up close, could see that the tie brought out the green in his eyes.

"*Kalimera*," they both said at once. She caught Niko's gaze sliding across her features.

"Olivia, this is Dimitrios. He's helping me at the bar today."

Dimitrios, dark and lanky, looking no more than twenty, raised his eyes and half-nodded, then continued working with a serious expression. It seemed they had all heard about her, as there was no need to explain who she was.

"Hi, Dimitrios. How can I help today, Niko?" she asked.

"People will start arriving after the church ceremony. Nina and a few others are inside, preparing. Nina will guide you."

When she walked into the kitchen, the noise that had been drowned outside by the music was almost deafening. Kostas, Elena, and Anastasia hollered instructions to each other over large metallic trays of prepared food. At the far side, Nina and three girls who looked like the female versions of Dimitrios were pouring serving sizes from huge plastic containers into small, ornamented meze dishes and bowls. Olivia had met one of the girls, Althea, the evening before.

"Olivia." Nina got up and welcomed her with kisses on both cheeks. "Join us. These are Angie, Althea, and Amara."

The three girls looked like triplets and their names made it even more confusing. Olivia hoped she would remember who was who. They, too, nodded at her as if they had been briefed about her.

"Sit here," Nina instructed. "We'll continue preparing, and the girls will start placing them on the tables."

Like a well-oiled machine, the girls got up, took out trays, loaded the ready dishes on them, and from that moment on, a runway of back and forth from the kitchen to the front had been established.

Once they were left to themselves, Nina continued to defy the tight-lipped tradition of the family. Even the frequent reappearance of the girls didn't deter her. Only when addressed by one of her parents or aunt, did she stop to breathe.

Amidst all the chatter, Olivia learned that Niko had a younger sister who lived in Athens with her family, as well as an older brother. Looking over Olivia's head at her parents and aunt, who were debating something regarding a large steaming clay pot, Nina whispered, "Their parents died a few years ago. A terrible car accident. A shock to everyone."

That piece of information had Olivia shoot a glance up from the dish she was filling, and a serving spoon of tzatziki spilled on the table.

Nina, returning her gaze, pressed her lips with a *terrible, right?* expression.

No wonder Niko didn't want to talk about his family when she had asked him. She figured she now knew why he had come back to the island after years abroad and had taken over the taverna.

"Niko is great," Nina went on. "How he stepped in with the taverna. My parents insist on helping him. My mother and his mother were cooks here before, so my mother wanted to continue. She doesn't want to retire, and my father helps when he can. He's a mechanic; he has a garage, but he comes here almost every day."

"And what about you?" Olivia asked.

"Oh, I help only on special occasions. Niko insists on paying not just my mother but also my father, but I don't let him pay me for this. I love doing it. Easier than being a teacher sometimes." Nina chuckled. "He brings my kids presents from Athens almost every month. That's enough for me."

Asking about Thalia after that—the only topic Nina left out—didn't sound relevant or tactful.

The next hour allowed less talk as they all carried large trays together and placed them on several long tables, set in a buffet-style.

By the time they finished, loud honking sounds were heard from outside.

"They're here," Nina said excitedly, as the girls and the older folk spoke in fast outbursts of Greek.

Olivia saw Niko and Dimitrios at the bar. Thanks to Nina, she now knew that Dimitrios was the brother of two of the girls, who were one year apart in age, and a cousin of the third girl, and that they were all related to Niko. The family wasn't oblivious to the similarity between the girls that were nicknamed "the triplets."

Niko, Elena, and Kostas greeted the first arrivals at the entrance, while the triplets showed people to their seats.

In a hectic half-hour, the place filled with two hundred guests, not including the bride and groom, who were almost the last to arrive.

"This is a small wedding," Nina commented. "We usually have more."

Having never been in a non-American-styled wedding, Olivia watched everything with immense interest. The older people were dressed as people usually dressed for church, but a few of the younger folk were in stilettos, very short or very long sequin or sheen dresses, and fancy suits or tuxedoes for the men. The bride and groom themselves were beautifully yet more modestly dressed.

"Those are from the mainland," Nina whispered to her as they passed together by a table of loud guests on the way to the kitchen to fetch meze refills. "They think they're in a movie."

Drinks were served at the bar and tables, and she saw Niko, Kostas, and Dimitrios move between the bar and the storeroom at the back of it.

The music was local and loud and, at some point, while the guests were busy eating, Nina touched her elbow and hinted for her to follow her to the kitchen. There, they sat at the side table and quickly ate from pre-arranged plates that awaited the staff.

There were no speeches made, as Olivia had been used to see in weddings, but after the first course was finished, a few people, both old and young, whom she had seen sneaking out before, entered, dressed in traditional clothing. The men wore what looked like white pantihose and skirts, blouses under brown leather vests, and slippers with a pompon at the toes. The women wore colorful dresses and aprons. To the sound of loud cheers, they entered in a row, their arms on each other's shoulders. In the space left especially between the guests' tables and the buffet, they performed a dance that Olivia thought was Zorba's dance, though she didn't recognize the tune.

The seated guests cheered and clapped, and when the music reached a fast-paced part, some joined the dance, calling, "*Opa.*" A few approached the bridal party and pulled them up to dance, as well. Olivia had only ever seen these Greek dances in movies. This was like the more beautiful, live version of *My Big Fat Greek Wedding*.

A few men got down on one knee while the bride and groom danced in the middle and drinks were shoved into their hands. "*Yamas,*" a mass of voices cheered when they downed the content of their glasses.

"I'll take the girls to clear the dishes from the tables, and you go with Dimitrios to pick up the empty bottles and take them back to the bar, okay?" Nina's voice startled Olivia.

"Sure," she replied.

Following Dimitrios, she slithered behind the dancing lines and picked up empty bottles and glasses, placing them in specially divided boxes that were much more convenient than trays.

Niko, at the bar, smirked at her. "Everything okay? You don't regret it?" he asked, raising his voice over the commotion.

"No, of course not! It's great."

"We have enough hands here if you're tired," he said.

"No, I don't mind the work, and I love seeing all this." She gestured with her head toward the dancing that went on not far from them.

"We dance better when we want to and not when we're expected." He winked, reminding her of their conversation at the Corfu Town taverna. "It will carry on till late," he then added, taking a plastic box from Dimitrios and placing it behind him in a pile.

Olivia's eyes washed over him. The way he moved made it hard to resist staring at him.

"That's okay. It's not like I have something else to do, and it's really lovely," she half-yelled so he would hear her.

"Okay. Make sure you take breaks," he said, his eyes penetrating hers.

She wondered if it was him being a caring boss to all the staff or was it him being a friend to her since she was a stranger among them. Either way, it all added up to Nina's account of him and her own impression.

After the main dish was served, Olivia was surprised to see a small live band consisting of two bouzouki players and an accordionist playing next to the impromptu dance floor.

Those who had finished their food got up and danced the Sirtaki-style dance again.

Clearing the dishes this time required Olivia, Nina, and the girls to zigzag between and behind the lines of dancers. The buffet trays were covered, but clean plates were placed near them so that the guests could refill whenever the dancing made them hungry again.

In the bathroom, Olivia found one of the sisters cleaning and refilling the toilet paper and paper towels. Washing her face and wetting her hair a bit so she could redo her tight bun, Olivia looked at her flushed face in the mirror and realized she hadn't thought about Seattle, the conference, Doreen, or anything else during the last six hours. She was so absorbed, and felt so much like a part of it all, that it was as if she had always been there and nothing else existed.

After cleaning her eyeglasses, she went to sit at the bar. Both Niko and Dimitrios seemed to be outside, as the back door was left open. Kostas leaned against the far end of the bar, watching the scene, wiping his forehead with a napkin.

The live band was now the main focus, and men and women danced in rows. Olivia's feet automatically tapped the bar stool to the rhythm of the music.

At certain points, everyone, even those in short sequin dresses, was down on one knee, clapping around one person who danced in the middle, arms spread wide, staggering around. Every now and then, they would swap places and someone else got to be in the middle to the cheers of the others. It seemed that each of them invented their own steps; some better than others.

"*Zeibekiko*," a male voice next to her said.

Olivia pivoted on the wooden bar stool to find Niko standing to her right.

"Some call it The Drunkard's dance," he explained.

"You have to be drunk?"

"No." He snickered. "You just have to be in a relevant mood. Sad or happy, it doesn't matter."

They watched the dancers, and Olivia chuckled to herself when Nina, her heavy braid bouncing on her shoulder, joined a row of dancers. The music became faster-paced and more people joined in.

Perplexed, she beheld the line that included Nina dancing its way toward the bar. "*Yamas*," Niko called, raising a glass of cloudy liquid, then emptying it.

"Nikos," several people called and, before she had a chance to digest it, Niko was swept away by the row that reached them and continued without stopping to the dance floor.

She found herself laughing, covering her mouth and nose with her hands, as she watched Niko dance with the rest. He blended in so naturally. But shouts of "Nikos," which she guessed was the more traditional way to pronounce his name, had the others in the row kneel in a circle around him, leaving him the only one standing. With his arms spread, legs somewhat bent, he danced as if the rhythm of the music coursed through him.

Sometimes almost kneeling, then rising to the cheers of those around him, he looked absolutely gorgeous. At some point, he loosened his tie and took it off and, to the applause of the kneeling folk, handed it to another man, who took it and replaced him in the center, while Niko kneeled on one knee and clapped for him. Olivia found herself staring at him.

He must have felt her eyes on him because he slightly turned his head and met her gaze. Olivia inhaled, holding the air in. Only when a small smile crossed Niko's features, she exhaled and smiled back.

Dimitrios and Kostas manned the bar and served cold drinks to the thirty guests who plodded toward them.

"We have to serve dessert, or they'll never leave," Nina said, slightly panting, as she came to call Olivia to the kitchen.

On each table, they placed carved watermelon; a plate of loukoumades, which Nina explained was fried dough filled with cream; bowls of yogurt, fresh fruits, and homemade jam; and ravani, a syrupy semolina cake with orange zest, served with ice cream.

Most of the work now moved to the dishwasher staff behind the kitchen. Elena and her sister left, and Nina's husband arrived with their kids and was seated at one of the tables.

"Call me if you need anything. I'm right over there," Nina told Olivia before joining them.

Olivia went back to the kitchen for a short break with one of the girls, who was the opposite of Nina when it came to chattiness.

When they emerged again, Nina's estimation had been proven when a group of older people and a family with small children greeted a goodbye on their way out, carrying the flower centerpieces from their tables.

It was easier to clear the dessert dishes, and the three girls did most of the work. After a while, Olivia went to sit with Nina. One of her boys was flumped on a chair, his head resting on his mother's lap.

"Should we do anything else?" Olivia asked.

"Not right now. Drink something."

"Thanks." Looking around, Olivia found a clean glass and poured herself red wine. "I enjoyed today. It was interesting. Thanks for being my guide."

"Anytime." Nina tapped her palm affectionately over Olivia's arm. "It's all family here."

"Are you and Niko related to the bride or groom?"

"No, but we know their family."

"Niko danced beautifully," Olivia ventured to say.

"Yes." Nina's gaze was on the dance floor, watching, like Olivia, the bride and groom dancing together inside a large circle of people. "They say the Zeibekiko is a dance of a man who lost something important, who was defeated and uses the dance to shed his sorrow and find his place again. That's why it doesn't have set steps. Anyone who needs to dance it makes it his own."

Olivia tore her eyes from the dance floor and stared at Nina, whose eyes were still on the newlyweds. She didn't expect such a poignantly beautiful explanation from this younger woman, whom she thought was a nice, chatty village teacher.

Returning her gaze to the dance floor, Olivia spotted the top of Niko's head behind the rows of dancers, and her heart skipped a beat. She swallowed and smoothed a probing hand over her hair.

Niko crossed the floor over to them. She readjusted her eyeglasses, wondering why her palms sweated. He stopped before them, honey-green eyes over a black shirt with the two top buttons open.

"Niko, I told two of the girls to leave. They'll come back later to undress the tables," Nina opened in English. "They know the work, and it's much easier than to prepare the tables," she added an aside to Olivia.

"I trust you, Nina," he responded.

He then looked at Olivia. "Everyone dances at Greek weddings. If you want to try it, now's the time before they change the music to Beyonce."

"Yes! You have to," Nina urged.

"Thanks, but I wouldn't know how." Olivia tightened her grip around the stem of the wineglass.

"There's nothing to know," Nina retorted.

"Oh, I've seen you both dance. You know what you're doing," she said, her eyes on Niko. She hoped he couldn't tell that she meant mostly him.

He reached out his hand to her. "Come on; I'll show you. Nina, come with us."

"I can't." She pointed at the child's head in her lap. Her husband was among the dancers.

Olivia took Niko's outstretched hand, and he pulled her to stand.

She looked back at Nina. "Don't laugh."

With her hand held in Niko's, he led her to the packed floor. To the cheers of those close to them who called his name, they joined the end of one of the rows. He rested his arm on the shoulders of the man to his left and wrapped his other around Olivia's shoulders. Since she was shorter, her arm was splayed mostly across his upper back, her palm gripping his shoulder. Her right arm was instinctively sent to the side to balance herself as she closed the row.

The music was fast-paced, and Olivia mimicked the steps of the others, hoping she wasn't just kicking her legs erratically because her attention was divided. She was all too aware of Niko's proximity and touch.

Glancing over at Nina, Olivia was relieved when the younger woman put her right hand across her heart and smiled approvingly.

She turned toward Niko and found herself staring into his face as he shifted his head in her direction at the exact same moment. He was so close that she could smell his breath and the mix of aftershave and masculine earthiness. A wisp of dark hair fell on his forehead, creating a mesmerizing frame to his eyes and accentuating his sun-kissed skin.

At some point, she wasn't sure if her feet moved her to the fast beat of the music or if she was carried by the row of dancers and Niko. She couldn't match the speed and heard herself laughing, heaving. Her heart raced, and she could feel her hair loosening its shackles. She didn't care; it could tousle and frizz as long as this exhilarating dance would continue.

At the peak of the rhythm, a few bouzouki notes slowed, and then the dance ended. Everyone cheered and clapped. She found herself in front of Niko, both panting and chuckling, their eyes locked together. Like memory foam, her body still bore the feeling of his arm across her shoulders and the way the side of his body pressed against hers.

In the background, the music changed. Recorded pop music that she didn't recognize replaced the live band.

"You got in at the best part," Niko said, bringing his mouth closer to her ear. "Now that they've gratified their parents, it'll be regular club music until the end." With his hand on her back, he escorted her back to Nina.

"You did great, Olivia," Nina squealed, stroking her son's hair. How the child could sleep in this raucous, Olivia couldn't fathom.

Niko handed her a glass of water, remaining standing while she took a seat next to Nina.

"Thanks." She met his gaze, her fingers lightly brushing his as she took it from him.

At nearby tables, groups of older people, holding the flowery centerpieces, took leave.

"The triplets will finish up," Nina informed. Indicating toward the bar, she added, "My father left. Dimitrios is there."

Olivia looked up. Niko's gaze was still on her. "Can I do something?" she asked.

"No, you're fine," he said.

"I'm here to work," she teased with a tilt of her head.

He hesitated. "You can help close the bar."

Following Niko across the taverna took longer than she expected. People stopped him, thanked him, and patted him on the back. She noticed the side-glances they saved for her. Twice, people he spoke to nodded at her after Niko said something, so she figured they asked and he explained who she was. She smiled back.

At the bar, Dimitrios toweled wet glasses, fresh from dishwashing, and held a spirited conversation with a group of young women and men who rested on the high bar stools.

"Well, *he's* busy," Niko joked, cocking his head toward Dimitrios. "You can help me with those. They're not heavy." He pointed at piles of trays, closed boxes, and crates that belonged in the storage room behind the bar or outside, where the vendors' vans would pick them up the next day.

Going back and forth, Olivia noticed that the party was becoming much smaller. Most of the tables were empty, and the three girls were clearing them now with Dimitrios's help. The music's loud bass pounded, coursing through her. The bride, groom, and their friends dominated the dance floor, while their parents sat together at the long, decorated table along the window. Nina and her family occupied another table.

When the last box was placed in the storage room, Olivia straightened up to find Niko waiting for her. She thought he would turn and they would leave, but they just stood there, facing each other.

"Thanks for letting me be a part of this today," she said, feeling her breath shallowing.

"Thank *you* for offering and working for free." He smiled.

She laughed. "Thank *you* for letting me stay at the house for free and for not letting me pay for anything. Maybe you planned it all along—that I'd work."

"How did you know?" he quipped, but the smile started fading from his face, and she felt that the distance between them was somehow diminishing.

"It was fun. I enjoyed it. I didn't think about … not even once."

"Good." His voice was a decibel lower. The rasp in it and the way he held her gaze, towering a head above her, made that one word sexier than any sleek speech.

Before she knew what she was doing, Olivia rose to her feet and bumped her face awkwardly with Niko's. It was supposed to be a kiss, but her eyeglasses got in the way and hit his nose, while her own nose crashed against his mouth.

If he was surprised, he didn't disclose it. He stood still, didn't falter or sway, as if he just tolerated it aloofly.

Regret flashed inside her. She pulled back just an inch, afraid to meet his gaze.

Niko sent his hands to gently hold her biceps, then distanced her from him. His gaze skimmed over her face, sending Olivia's heart rate through the roof. He then reached one hand and removed her eyeglasses without taking his eyes off hers. Holding the plastic frame, he bent his head, and she managed to expel a nervous breath before his lips landed in the right place—on hers.

Chapter 8

His lips felt soft against hers, then fiercer when she opened her mouth to his and he deepened the kiss. She reached out to hold him.

Niko raked his hands up from her biceps to her neck. Then, with his free hand, he released the scrunchie that kept her rebellious hair in place and weaved his fingers into her loosened curls, nestling her head in his palm and melding their mouths further together.

He smelled like the beach and tasted sweet and spicy. It was new and different. Most times, Jeff tasted like toothpaste—cool and sanitized. But Niko tasted of spiced honey and warmth. The way he held her against him sent warm waves down her body.

The noise from the taverna was lost on Olivia. All she heard were Niko's and hers huffed breaths and the little moan that escaped her throat into Niko's mouth.

She roamed her hands across the solid plains of his chest and shoulders. His warmth radiated through the fabric of his shirt, and she wanted to take it off and discover what he felt like underneath it.

For the first time in years, her entire body hummed just from a kiss.

But it wasn't just a kiss. Niko made her body feel like it was foam that would melt in his arms. It wasn't just a kiss. It was also her acting on a whim, throwing caution and calculations to the wind.

A loud noise of metal hitting asphalt outside startled them. Olivia became at once aware of the loud bass and beat of the music coming from the taverna.

Niko's hands still enveloped her, and their bodies still touched. She hated whoever had made that sudden racket outside.

"Your glasses," Niko rasped, handing her the blue plastic frame.

"Thanks." She slipped her hands from his shoulders as she stepped back and put her glasses back on, sending a hand that felt like clay to smooth over her ruffled hair.

Niko stroked her arm, pressing his lips together, then turned and walked outside. A second later, she heard him speaking to someone in Greek. It sounded like Dimitrios.

Going back into the taverna, Olivia approached Nina, who was getting ready to leave.

"Are we done here?" Olivia had to shout this into Nina's ear.

"Yes. There's not much left to do. You can go."

Thanking each other, they hugged.

Olivia looked around. Niko was nowhere to be seen. "Tell Niko I said bye if you see him, okay?"

Nina patted Olivia's forearm in response.

~~~~~~~~~~~~~~~~~~~~~~~~~~~~~~~

Leaving through the front door and taking a few steps away from the taverna, Olivia filled her lungs with the clear evening air. Her ears still pounded from the music, and her heart thumped in her chest but for a different reason.

As she turned the corner into the lane of houses, the dark blue sea, and the moon and lights that reflected on its surface, pacified the gush of blood in her veins.

Lying on the sofa, Olivia knew she would feel the result of the day's work in her muscles tomorrow. Her body wasn't used to this; her gym membership had been wasted in the last year. Her body also wasn't used to the sensations that kissing Niko had awoken in her; sensations that weren't extinguished even an hour and a shower later.

To distract herself, she checked for messages on her phone. Finding almost none only served to remind her how much her world had narrowed down in just a few days. It was a strange feeling, and she was surprised that it wasn't a more painful one.

"Believe, Become, Belong" had been the mantra she had used with her clients. "*Create meaning and purpose for your employees to believe in, to belong to.*" It was a sentence from her intercepted speech. For a few hours today, she had experienced this more acutely working with Nina, Niko, and the others than she had in her time at Teamtastic.

She wanted more of this, still needed the timeout, and liked it here. She even thought to offer Niko her continued help. But, was she the type to do that and casually have a fling with him, too? Maybe yes. After all, she had known Niko for four days, and she wouldn't stay here long enough to develop real feelings. She had been with Jeff for almost a year before she felt she could say "I love you."

Besides, that kiss could be just a one-off, something they would both ignore. If he wouldn't make any reference to it, she wouldn't, either. It shouldn't be complicated, right?

Her muscles begging her to go to sleep spared Olivia from giving herself an honest answer.

~~~~~~~~~~~~~~~~~~~~~~~~~~~~~~~~~

She had overslept. Waking up, every muscle in her body reminded Olivia of the day before.

Walking the beautiful, empty alleys in the middle of a Monday, when the few people she passed by looked like they were in the middle of doing something, of living their normal lives, made her feel like the alien that she was.

Entering the taverna with a thrumming heart, she immediately saw Niko at the bar. He was with his back to the entrance. The place looked like no wedding had been held there the night before. Everything was back in its place.

"*Kalimera*," she greeted.

He turned, and her heart fluttered. "*Kalimera*."

They just stood there, looking at each other.

Two men at a nearby table, chatting amongst themselves, and the music playing in the background were the only interruption to the silence.

"I'll get you coffee," Niko was the first to speak.

"Thanks." *Oh no*. Even that one word sounded faltering in Olivia's own ears.

She sat on a bar stool, unwilling to sit as a guest at "her" table. Niko turned from the coffee-making spot and placed a steamy coffee cup in front of her.

True to her resolution, she forced herself to open. "Niko, I hope you won't think it presumptuous, but I have an idea." It was hard to look at him without being distracted by memories of how his lips felt on hers and how his body felt when she was pressed against it. "Nina told me that Elena is the cook, and that she only waits on tables because she doesn't want you to pay someone on slow days. How about if I do the waitressing job, instead?"

Niko chewed on his lower lip, quickly wetting it with his tongue. "You're offering to pay with work again. While we're not equipped to host tourists, we're happy to let friends stay. No need for payment." The honey-green eyes, reflecting the light that came in from the bright morning outside, were serious and sincere.

He spoke in plural, but Olivia knew he was referring to himself.

"I appreciate this, Niko. Really. You're too kind. But if *you* don't mind having more help, then *I'd* be more than happy to do it. Regardless of payment." She felt the warm flush washing over her face.

"Waiting on tables isn't the best touristic experience."

"I'm way past being a regular tourist."

"It's never too late. How long do you think you'll be doing this?"

She exhaled. His intention with that question was clear to her. "It might be just a week. I'll do it as long as I stay. If you don't mind letting me run

around here. It's just until I'm … ready to go back."
She had faltered again.

He didn't reply immediately. For Olivia, the moment of silence stretched forever. She shifted on her seat.

"What are you hiding from?" he finally asked.

"I'm not exactly hiding. I just … I need to … I left as one thing, and now I will be back as another. I know it sounds stupid. I'm still me." The last words were accompanied by a cackle. If this was a job interview and she was interviewing herself, she would turn herself down.

Niko placed his palm on the bar. "Okay."

"Okay, what?"

"Okay, you can work here if you want. But—"

"That's great! Thank you!" she cut in.

"You're offering again to work for free, so don't thank *me*." He chuckled.

"It's not for free, and if I have as much fun as I had yesterday, then *you're* paying me."

A smile appeared on Niko's face, and Olivia's face flushed again. The moment the words had come out of her mouth, she realized how they had sounded. From his expression, she knew he understood her original meaning as well as her alternate interpretation.

"You know what I mean," she mumbled.

"The wedding, of course," he said, saving her again from embarrassment.

She held her gaze as steady as she could on his face, keeping it from sliding down his body. He looked so good in the dark grey Henley shirt.

"You were saying that I can help here, but … and I didn't let you finish the sentence. What were you going to say?" She jolted herself out of the visuals that began playing in her mind of what he looked and felt like under those clothes. *If he won't refer to the kiss, I won't either*, she reminded herself.

"Oh, just that, although most people here understand some English, without knowing the language, it might be a bit hard for you to wait on tables. So, you can help Elena with other things, too. She could use help, but I'll let her decide with what."

Olivia's throat dried, and she felt her cheeks reddening yet again. Niko was right; this wasn't the work she had been used to, and this could be the only explanation for her missing such a glaring fact as the language barrier.

He might have noticed the alarm on her face, because Niko added, "She'd appreciate the help, don't get me wrong. I employ one of the triplets when there's pressure, but she's too stubborn to let me hire someone on a regular basis, and I don't want to argue with her." His tone and smile seemed aimed at making her feel included in the family banter.

"Okay."

She rested her hand on the bar, and Niko, without warning, put his palm on the back of hers. "Elena likes you. She'll be happy to hear you volunteered to help her."

Her eyes were glued to his palm covering hers.

Niko removed his hand, and she raised her eyes to glance at him. "She wouldn't mind that I'm not family?"

"She wouldn't, and I don't either. It'll be nice to have you here."

Olivia's mind went quickly over her encounters with Elena. They had hardly exchanged more than a few service or work-related words. She was too shy to ask now if Elena could handle English well. She trusted that Niko would have told her if that wasn't the case.

"When can I start?" she asked, instead.

"I'll go talk to Elena." He hesitated for a brief second. "If you want, the storage room could use some arranging after yesterday." From the look on his face, she knew they were both thinking the same thing.

Olivia got to her feet and went around into the bar area. Niko excused himself and left for the kitchen while she entered the storage room.

~~~~~~~~~~~~~~~~~~~~~~~~~~~~~~~~

"Elena was really happy to hear, and she's waiting for you in the kitchen." Niko's voice ran a warm shiver down Olivia's back.

She pivoted toward him. She had nearly finished arranging the storage room. While at it, she had taken the liberty to peek into the different boxes and rearrange a few shelves.

"Wow, you've been productive." He took a few steps into the room.

Olivia wiped her hands with a clean rag that she had hung on a hook off one of the shelves and followed his gaze. They were standing two feet apart, but it felt closer. "She's waiting for me?" she echoed.

Niko nodded. She had a feeling he had embellished Elena's reaction.

The room felt small with them at this proximity, and Olivia reminded herself that she didn't stay here for him or offered to work here because of him.

"I'd better go see what she wants me to start with." She sidestepped him, feeling his eyes following her, and a whiff of his clean, earthy scent reached her on the way out.

~~~~~~~~~~~~~~~~~~~~~~~~~~~~~~

Elena's English wasn't nearly as good as Niko's or Nina's, but they managed to understand each other well. She welcomed Olivia with a black apron, helping her tie it over her jeans, before showing her around the kitchen. At the front and on the balcony, she enumerated the tables. Olivia learned that "her" window table was numbered thirty-two.

Everything was freshly cooked and prepared the same day with only a few things lasting for more than one day. Most of the menu was permanent, but Elena made sure to add at least two different dishes every day. The busier days were Wednesday to Sunday and weddings, christenings, and other occasions occurred approximately once a month.

With hand gestures and pantomime to replace words and phrases she didn't know, Elena was able to give Olivia the full theoretical knowledge that she would need for the beginning. Beyond helping in the kitchen, they agreed that Olivia would serve the food, although Elena would take the orders from the tables, and that they would use a clockwise system to let Olivia know which guest ordered what.

Since the taverna boasted a family-like atmosphere, the service wasn't too formal. Plates and platters were carried by hand and not on trays, and the same was mostly true for drinks. As Olivia shadowed Elena during the day, her nervousness decreased. It wasn't a busy day, but with everything she had to learn, it had been just the right volume for a beginner.

Throughout, she had felt Niko's presence in the encouraging smiles that he gave her whenever she caught his eyes or the stealthy thumbs-up he gestured when she served her first table alone. She chuckled, remembering what he had told her about that specific gesture.

"You're doing great. And thank you. I can already see Elena running around a lot less," he said when she came to the bar to fetch drinks. "Are you sure you're okay, though?"

"I'm great," she replied. And she was. It was easy to get absorbed in this—sunlight instead of fluorescent, music instead of hushed offices, speaking informally to people instead of rambling in pretentious business lingo. Sure, she had spilled an ouzo shot on herself and stained her light pink top with sauce. For now, however, it felt good being there than anywhere else.

"We close early on Mondays. Not much action going after six. So, feel free to leave whenever you've had enough," Niko said.

When Elena left at around three p.m., Kostas arrived to replace her. Olivia couldn't fathom where Nina had gotten her chattiness from; Kostas was by far the least talkative of her relatives.

Olivia hung her apron on the kitchen's wall hook rail before six.

Kostas and Niko were both at the bar when she came to take leave.

"Ever tried ouzo with water?" Niko asked.

"Can't say I have."

Niko gestured with his hand toward the bar stools, and she took a seat, her muscles complaining at the change of posture.

Kostas muttered something and excused himself when Niko placed three shot glasses on the counter. He then discarded one glass and created a cloudy drink in the other two by mixing the liquids.

Niko handed her the drink and clinked his glass with hers. "*Yamas.*"

Olivia squinted her eyes and scrunched up her nose as the drink rolled on her tongue. "I still like rakomelo or just plain wine or beer better."

"If you stay long enough, you might learn to like it more."

They exchanged a glance.

Afraid she would inflate his words with more meaning, she moved to focus on the chalk handwritten menu behind him. "How does the work schedule usually go?"

"When the triplets work, their shifts are from eleven to five and five until closing, which is around eleven p.m. You've done a full shift today."

She returned her gaze to him and smoothed a hand over her hair. "Is there a preferred shift you'd like me to take?"

He gave her a few possibilities while ensuring she wasn't overcommitting. Then, winking, he added, "I don't know how long you'd stay, but the weekends are busier, and we even have tourists stopping by for lunch and dinner."

"Do you expect them to get by with no English menu or do you pretend you don't know English, hoping they'll go away?" She smirked and jutted her chin toward the menu.

"Depending on what they wear," he reciprocated.

She laughed, her heart beating faster.

Kostas, appearing from the back, deposited a large box of bottles on the floor with a grunt. Niko turned to him, and they exchanged a few sentences.

The moment was dispelled, and Olivia excused herself. She had passed a whole day in Niko's presence and was none the wiser about the passionate kiss they had shared the day before. Was he waiting for her to make a move, was he indifferent, was he used to kissing strangers in the storage room, or was he sparing her because he perceived that she was out of her depth?

~~~~~~~~~~~~~~~~~~~~~~~~~~~~~~~~

On the veranda, after a hot shower, Olivia watered the plants, using a large pitcher that she had found in one of the kitchen cabinets. She circled the house, watering the flowers and bushes that grew along the paved path.

"Damn," she hissed when her foot stumbled on what looked like a wooden ramp that was leaning against the house wall.

Returning to sit on the veranda, she massaged her foot and opened YouTube. A quick search resulted in several tutorials on the Greek alphabet. It bothered her all day that she couldn't read the menu and the notes that hung on the taverna's kitchen and bar walls. If she wanted to be of real help, she should at least be able to read the dishes' names.

Most of the letters were familiar from the distant past of math lessons or sorority symbols. She had never been in a sorority but knew the letters of a few. The tutorials jogged her memory and, by the time she went to bed, she had them all scribbled down on a piece of paper and memorized.

On the way to the bedroom, she stopped next to Thalia's large painting. Under the name in English, she could now recognize that what had looked like a strange O with a little shape in it was the Greek letter Theta, which was Thalia's initial. She wondered when the painter slash almost professor slash yoga instructor would be back from Mykonos. More than that, she wondered yet again what her connection to Niko really was.

On Tuesday morning, while eating a bowl of cereal that she had bought at the grocery store two days before, Olivia tried to open her Teamtastic Outlook account. A pang clenched her stomach when she realized it had been disabled. She pushed the half-finished bowl and opened her personal Gmail. A few emails from Doreen awaited, each carrying a different reminder of her termination—a final payslip, a tax form, and a letter of recommendation which didn't bear Teamtastic's logo, only Doreen's role and signature, which made Olivia appreciate Doreen a bit better, realizing that she probably had written it without approval.

Like someone looking for safe ground to step on after experiencing quicksand, Olivia marched toward Teresi's Taverna. There, she nodded and kalimera'd Kostas, who manned the bar, went straight into the kitchen, greeted Elena warmly, and put on the black apron.

She was about to go out of the kitchen when she turned on her heels instead and returned to the corner of the kitchen where the hook rack hung on the wall above an old cabinet that Nina and the others used to store their personal belongings while working. A laminated picture was pasted to the wall, probably one that had been taken in one of the events that had been held at the taverna. Niko, Nina, Kostas, Elena, her sister, the triplets, Dimitrios, and a few unfamiliar faces smiled at her. All around them, their names were written in different handwritings. Some, she could now read.

Taking a pen out of a basket that stood on top of the low cabinet, Olivia carefully added her name in

Greek letters at the bottom corner of the page over the lamination, where it could later be erased.

For two hours, she followed Elena's broken English instructions, learned how the most popular dishes were served—these were mainly the traditional meat and fish dishes that she herself had never tasted—and served them to a few tables, along with the drinks that Kostas prepared.

"How are you holding up?" Niko's voice surprised her from behind when she was stocking up shelves in the large fridge.

"Oh, hi." She had been keyed up to his arrival. "I'm great. I hope Elena thinks so, too."

"She does. I asked her." He smiled.

"Checking on your staff is important." She couldn't help but smile back.

He seemed to hesitate before he spoke next. "Listen, I have to fly to Athens today. Will you be okay here? You know you can stop this volunteering work anytime, right?"

"Athens?" she just said.

"Yes. I'll probably be back tomorrow."

She recalled Nina mentioned he visited his brother and sister in Athens every month, but this sounded like an unplanned trip.

"Don't worry about it. Elena is a great mentor. But, is everything okay?"

"Everything's fine. I'll see you tomorrow. Or the day after."

Niko left, and Olivia returned to stowing containers inside the fridge, chastising herself out of the heavier movements that her body suddenly exhibited.

"Olivia." His voice surprised her again, and she turned. "If you need anything, this is my phone number." Niko handed her a piece of paper with the number handwritten in blue pen.

"Thank you. I'll try not to burst any pipes at the house while you're gone," she bantered.

Niko chuckled, holding her gaze before exiting the kitchen.

~~~~~~~~~~~~~~~~~~~~~~~~~~~~~~~~~~

Unwilling to submit herself to idleness and taking advantage of the long daylight that June offered, Olivia used Google's advice and took a bus early that afternoon to Paleokastritsa.

The village bustled like a small town in comparison to Aleniki. She strolled its alleys that were packed with tourists and strewn with every shop conceivable that could entertain them. She found herself peering into tavernas and bars, comparing them to Niko's. Following the herds of tourists, she reached the beach.

A boardwalk over the impossibly turquoise water led to cruise boats. She bought a ticket and, for two hours, sailed along the coast. The view was breathtaking, and the sea was every shade of blue imaginable. They sailed along beaches, coves, cliffs, and natural grottoes.

A recorded guide educated the passengers about the history of the island and of the Paleokastritsa area with its Venetian and Adriatic Sea style architecture.

"A hundred kilometers that way, and we'll reach Italy," the captain himself pointed out through the speakers later. "Half that distance, and we'll reach Albania, and after that, Montenegro."

For some reason, watching the island from afar made Olivia's chest tighten as if she missed it.

Returning to the shore, she chose a cozy-looking taverna and ordered the vegetarian platter from the English picture menu that offered an eclectic variety of American and British dishes, in addition to the traditional Greek food. *The experience wasn't half as good as in Teresi's Taverna*, she thought with satisfaction as she ambled through the busy alleys later.

The snazzy summer dresses that smiled from every shop window tempted Olivia to make one more stop on the way to the bus. In addition to an A-shaped green dress and a wavy floral envelope dress, she bought another bra, a V-shaped, red shirt, and a simple one-piece red swimsuit. "Red is good for blondes, even your ash," an overly honest saleswoman had advised in Olivia's first girls-only mall tour in the seventh grade." Back home, she would need several shopping sprees to have chosen all these garments, especially the swimsuit, but here, it was all done in less than an hour. She wasn't sure why; she was still the same Olivia. She also wasn't sure why she threw in a pair of black jeans, as well, except that it might be a good idea to have comfortable yet presentable pants in case she would be part of the taverna staff in another wedding.

Practicalities like flights, luggage, and realistic timelines were temporarily stored at the back of her mind.

Chapter 9

The few old women and men who sat on straw stools outside their houses daily, chatting together, recognized and greeted her as Olivia made her way toward the taverna the next day. Surprised, she smiled and replied with *kalimera* and *efkharisto poly*. She didn't understand the enthusiastic flow that followed in reply but figured they appreciated that she knew the basic words.

Maybe it was her imagination, but Elena and Kostas seemed somewhat dejected that day. To her question, "Is Niko back?" Elena replied with a laconic, "Tomorrow."

She was pleasantly surprised again when a few regulars knew her name and chatted to her in simple English. Two asked her where Niko was, and another, Darius, an older man who had coffee at the taverna every day, asked if she had moved to Corfu. As she replied that this was a temporary stay, she had a feeling that he had already known this and had only asked to gauge her reaction.

Though the day flew by, there were moments when, looking over at the bar and seeing only Kostas or Dimitrios, who came with his sister, Althea, to help in the afternoon, made Olivia's stomach feel hollow. When another one of the triplets arrived after Elena had left, Olivia hung her apron on the hook in the kitchen and returned to the house.

It wasn't that she missed Niko—how could you miss someone you have only known for a week—it was just that she needed some quiet time to herself, to think about what was next for her, to plan her return.

But she didn't do any of that. Instead, she ate the Greek delicacies that Elena had urged her to take in the plastic containers that Olivia had washed and returned. She then texted her mother, brother, and Daria the selfies that she had taken the day before.

~~~~~~~~~~~~~~~~~~~~~~~~~~~~~~

The afternoon gave way to evening, but there was still enough light for Olivia to descend the veranda steps and stroll the olive grove behind the house. She crossed it to the neighboring lemon orchard and saw glimpses of the sea glinting in the gaps among the trees.

When a text message landed on her phone with a *ping*, Olivia extracted it from the back pocket of her jeans, not expecting to see the name that appeared on the screen.

Jeff.

She had hardly thought of him since the day of the conference. She had bigger issues to deal with, though it bothered her that he had partaken in the humiliation, given that Daria's message disparaged his performance in the sack. With a sinking heart, she read his message.

"Sorry I didn't check on you before. It was pretty horrible what happened to you. I guess I was too

mad at what Daria wrote. Was it really that bad? I didn't think it was."

She hesitated. "*I'm sorry you were dragged into this.*"

"*Isn't it five a.m. for you?*" he wrote.

"*I'm still in Greece.*"

"*What are you still doing there?*"

"*What people usually do in Greece,*" she lied.

There was a pause. "*Jeff is typing*" appeared and disappeared several times. She was back on the veranda when his message finally arrived.

"*I need to be in Seattle sometime soon. Can we meet?*"

Now it was her turn to hesitate. *Why?* was what she wanted to type. Did he want to meet to get an answer to his question regarding Daria's description of their sex life?

"*If I'm back by then,*" she ended up typing.

Another ping. Olivia opened the message. It was a picture of an empty road with a quote typed across. "*To know the road ahead, ask those coming back. A Chinese proverb.*"

Olivia sighed. For months, she had vacillated whether letting Jeff move to Boston without her had been right. This was their first contact since they had finalized the split.

Could you miss someone you have known a few days more than someone you had been with a decade?

The busier hours of lunch gone by, Olivia took her break at a window table. Clearing and wiping it after she had finished, she sang along to the music that played in the background. Some of the more catchy songs had become familiar, though she invented Gibberish that sounded like the Greek words in the repeated choruses.

"*Alla mou len ta matia sou*," a voice startled her.

She spun around. "Hey." She couldn't stop the smile that spread on her face or the acceleration of her heart. "Am I butchering the song?"

"Just a little." Niko smiled.

"You're back." She stood up and stifled an urge to throw her arms around him.

"Yes."

It didn't seem like he was going to say more. They just stood there.

"What do the words mean?" she ended up asking.

"*Your eyes tell me different things*."

Olivia swallowed. God, she loved hearing his accent rolling the words and the way the "S" sounded soft in his mouth. It made her heart beat even faster, remembering that mouth against hers.

"I like this music."

"That's rebetiko. It's like the blues of Greek music."

Were they really standing there, discussing music?

"When will you have more dancing here?"

"It depends on the atmosphere. Last Wednesday, there was dancing here at night. Someone started, and it rolled from there."

"Last Wednesday, I landed in Corfu without my luggage. Maybe I should have come here then instead of the next day." It was hard to believe it had been only a week. Then again, it was encouraging to think it was only a week.

"Maybe." He paused. "I have to drive up to Sidari to drop something off. Since you've hardly seen the island, would you like to come with me?"

"Oh. Um, I don't know. Will Elena be okay?"

"Althea is coming soon."

"I took a trip to Pali-something two days ago."

"Paleokastritsa?"

"Yes, that." *What was she doing?* "But I'd love to see more of the island."

"Okay. We'll leave in thirty minutes."

Olivia made a stop at the bathroom. She untied her tightly-made bun, but her hair refused to settle, so she tied it back. *It's not a date*, she reminded herself while applying the rose-tinted Chapstick.

Out through the back door, they reached the alley behind the taverna where Niko's green car parked.

"You want the top off?" he asked. Before her mind could go wild with guesses, Niko gestured with his head toward the car's roof.

She hoped she wasn't the color of her red scrunchie when she called, "The roof. Yes!"

Niko pressed a button, and the roof folded.

"*It's not practical; it's for showing off*," Olivia recalled Jeff's criticism of a friend who had bought a convertible. Back then, she had shrugged, having no opinion one way or the other. However, in the warmth of a June afternoon on a Greek island, under brilliant blue skies and with turquoise sea as far as the eye could see, the ride with the roof off made Olivia feel like throwing her arms up in the air and howling.

They drove up to Sidari, which Olivia read on Google was a coveted resort destination on the northwest tip of the island. The views on the way were as gorgeous as the ones she had seen on her afternoon trip two days earlier. She could see why Aleniki was considered to be off the tourist trail, though it was as beautiful to her now.

Niko pointed, explained, and added anecdotes about places they drove by. She listened with interest, though the way the wind had swept his hair off his forehead and clung his shirt to his shoulders and chest made it hard to concentrate.

"Where are we going to in Sidari?" she asked.

"You'll see. I have to drop off samples I brought from Athens."

"How was Athens?"

"Good."

She looked at his profile. His eyes were hidden behind sunglasses, but the twitch in his jaw was visible.

Niko returned her gaze. "Do you want me to put the roof back on?"

"No, I love it." The wind had loosened wisps of ash-blonde hair from its scrunchy prison and covered her eyeglasses in a thin layer of dust, but Olivia didn't care. Not as long as these heart-widening views of blue and green mixed with the soft pinks, peaches, and yellows of the houses flew by.

"*Melitsa*," she read out loud the signpost written in Greek that marked their arrival at the outskirts of Sidari.

From the corner of her eyes, she caught Niko snapping his head to watch her.

"You can read Greek?"

"Not exactly. I taught myself the letters, but I don't understand the words."

"You taught yourself the letters?" A strange expression crossed Niko's face, as if his features had softened.

"I wanted to be able to read the menu Elena chalks up."

"And can you read it?"

"Yes."

He threw a gaze at her before focusing again on the narrower lanes of the village center.

Set right on the beach, the place was bustling with people and small shops. The colorful houses on the side street that Niko parked on were covered in climbing bougainvilleas.

Extracting a big, flat box from the trunk, Niko motioned Olivia toward one of those houses.

A door was opened at the side of the building, and she followed him in. A steady hum of machines and people speaking was heard from farther down a corridor.

"*Ya, theia*," Niko called.

A woman that Olivia estimated was about sixty years old, tall and smiling, emerged from a door and rushed toward Niko with an effusion of Greek. Niko shifted the box he was carrying so she could hug him.

"*Theia*, this is Olivia. She's staying in Corfu for a few days and helping us at the taverna," he said in English.

"Olivia, this is my *theia*, Katerina. She's my father's and Kostas' sister and the owner of this factory."

As the two shook hands, Katerina warmly covering Olivia's palm with her other hand, Niko half-whispered to Olivia, "*Theia* means aunt in Greek."

Olivia smiled at his successful guess of her momentary confusion.

They followed Katerina into a large hall filled with rows of sewing machines, operated by several women and a few men.

"My aunt sells luxury, handmade textiles to the best hotels on several islands. And to me, for my best taverna on this island."

Laughing, Niko evaded a playful smack that his aunt sent toward his arm.

"Don't listen to him," Katerina said, turning to Olivia. "It *is* the best taverna on the island."

"It is," Olivia replied, smiling.

"You, go and put that box in the sample room," Katerina ordered Niko while taking Olivia's hand in hers and drawing her for a short tour around the main hall of her factory.

After name-dropping hotel chains and boasting beautiful textile examples, Katerina asked, "Are you Niko's friend from abroad?"

Olivia had a feeling Katerina had an aim in sending Niko away and keeping her by her side.

"No, I met him here, at the taverna. I was looking for a place to rent for a few days and he offered the house your family has."

"It was his parents' house."

"I didn't know that."

"So, you work at the taverna?"

"I help. It gives me something to do while I'm here. And Niko refuses to take money from me."

"Yes, that's Niko. You know, he used to send me unique fabrics when he lived abroad. Now, every month, he brings me whatever I ask for from Athens."

Olivia only managed to nod before the aunt continued. "We are all happy he came back. Niko is like my brother, his father, may he rest in peace. His father was … you know those people who everyone center around them? That was my brother. That's Niko. They don't even notice they do it. It just happens. Niko, he had a great future in diplomacy because of it. But he's happier here. He wasn't happy there, though I loved having a nephew in the capitals of the world." She stopped to draw a quick breath then continued, crossing herself. "My husband, may he rest in peace, too, wasn't like that at all. I think I am more like that …"

Olivia discovered where Nina got her talkativeness from. She didn't manage to insert more than two words into the conversation before Niko turned up.

"She shared her grief over my lost career?" he asked as they crossed a small square on the way back to the car.

"She mentioned it." Olivia chuckled.

122

Near the car, Niko wavered. "Do you want to get something to drink on the beach?"

"I'd love to. But I read this one is a touristic hotspot."

Niko laughed. "Didn't Katerina tell you all about me living in Hague for three years? I love the noise, too, but I like to be able to go home to a quiet place after spending time in the noisy ones. Are you worried about my well-being?"

It was Olivia's turn to laugh.

~~~~~~~~~~~~~~~~~~~~~~~~~~~~~~~

They left the car there and walked down a road that led to a promenade that stretched along a sandy beach. Breathtakingly beautiful, it was strewn with tavernas and beach bars. Thatched umbrellas and sunbeds were neatly organized on the sand, and a mixture of languages was heard everywhere.

"I'll have a watermelon margarita, *parakalo*." Olivia smiled at the waitress while closing the menu. Sitting on the balcony of a beach bar with Niko, this drink would seal the experience.

Niko ordered coffee and, as soon as the waitress left, they both spoke together.

"So, now you met all my family in Corfu," Niko opened right when she did, "So, that's your parents' house."

They looked at each other and laughed.

"You go first," she said.

"Yes, that was my parents' house. I was just thinking that now you met all my family in Corfu, but I know nothing about yours. Don't they miss you?"

She shrugged. "I have a brother who lives in Cincinnati with his family, and my parents in Seattle. Not much to tell."

"What about friends?"

She told him briefly about Daria and mentioned Jeff and their breakup over his move to Boston.

"Do they know what happened and why you stayed and what you do?"

"Daria knows, my parents don't. They wouldn't understand, but I'll tell them soon."

"That you volunteer to work in a taverna?"

"That, too. If someone had told me that last week, I wouldn't have believed it myself."

"Do you know how long you'll stay? You learned the Greek alphabet. That's serious."

He smiled, but Olivia felt a little panicky pinch in her chest.

"I like working in the taverna while I'm here. Unless you don't want me there, which I can understand. I put you in an awkward position."

"That's not at all what I meant." His expression softened again. "Weren't you in HR and good at reading people? Can't you tell that we like having you here?"

Maybe if you didn't speak in plural, Olivia thought.

A waiter arrived with their drinks, a blessed interruption.

She took a sip from her glass. "It's really good. Want to try?" She handed him her glass.

Niko took a sip. "It's good. I make these, too, though there's not much demand from the locals." He handed her the glass. "Okay, your turn."

"The house. You said it would just stay closed up if I wasn't there; why? It's so beautiful. Why aren't you using it? Because of your parents?" She hoped he would open up even as little as she had.

"Nina probably told you about the car accident. When I moved back here, I remodeled it, but after some time, I bought the apartment above the taverna."

"Were there bad memories?"

"No. There were regrets. The taverna was enough of a reminder, and I wanted to go home to a place that wouldn't serve as another. I don't feel the same anymore, but I got used to the apartment."

"Reminder of what?"

"Of missing out; of focusing on the wrong thing, chasing the next role, achieving it and still feeling unfulfilled; forgetting what really mattered."

She recalled Nina's explanation about the Zeibekiko—a dance of a man who lost something, who knew defeat and had to rebuild himself.

"What happened, Niko?" she dared.

Niko averted his gaze toward the sea. "I was too busy to come home for holidays, weddings, christenings. I ended up coming home for a double funeral. I spent two months here, and everyone around me had so much more meaning and was so much happier than me, though I finally landed the role I wanted and was living the high life. Suddenly, going places, being in places, didn't seem important, interesting, fulfilling." He shrugged. "I went back to the Netherlands and to work, but it wasn't *it* anymore. I kept missing what I found here. So, I quit and took over the taverna."

"And are you happy now?"

"Yes. I got off that crazy train, and I don't miss it. I know that, to others, living in a small village and running a taverna doesn't sound exciting. Maybe it's not. But I'm not looking for excitement. At least, not that kind. I found my place. I have a purpose, people I love. I travel once a year, and that's enough for me."

Olivia stared at him. Here was a living incarnation of everything she had lectured on—believe, become, belong.

He let his gaze travel until he stared at the sea again.

She wanted to get out of her chair and go hug him. She sucked in her bottom lip, wanting to know more but hesitating if to push it. "What about relationships?" To her, that question brought their kiss from five days earlier to stand tangibly between them, and she wondered if he felt it, too.

"I didn't have much time for that, either. I had a few"—Niko tilted his head, as if weighing his words—"medium-term relationships in my almost fifteen years abroad, but nothing worth giving up the job for whenever I moved." A tentative smile appeared on his face, and Olivia wondered if that was a reference to her mentioning her split-up with Jeff, although she hadn't delved into the details.

"And since?" she asked.

"Nothing serious."

"Short and to the point."

"When I came back here, everyone my age was either already married or related to me."

They both laughed.

Everyone *his age*. "What about Thalia? Is she related to you?"

Niko parked his gaze on her. In the sunlight, the honey in his eyes was more prevalent. "No. She's just a friend. She's from the mainland, but her parents had a house in Corfu. She travels a lot; we don't see much of her."

Olivia found herself biting the inside of her bottom lip. He had spoken in the plural again.

"If you're asking if I'm involved with her, then the answer is no. We used to, once, after I came back. But not since."

He didn't specify what "we used to" meant, but it was obvious that the missing part of the sentence was "sleep together." On one hand, that wasn't a surprise. She had sensed an energy between them. On the other hand, Niko verifying it caused her stomach to drop.

"Do you want to go down to the beach? We're so close," he said, maybe in an effort to divert the conversation.

Like in Corfu Town, he didn't let her pay.

A few steps only separated them from the sand. Shoes in hands, they treaded between families and gangs of selfie-taking twenty-somethings toward the water. Niko rolled up his jeans, she was in her new green dress, and in they went, calf-high. The water was refreshingly cold and so clear that Olivia could see tiny, grey fish escaping them.

"How was it growing up here?" she asked.

"When I wasn't in school or helping my parents in the taverna or at home, I was always on the beach with my friends. Sometimes, even instead of school or helping out at home. We met tourists and had fun."

Though Olivia couldn't see his eyes under the sunglasses that he had put back on, the laughter lines around his eyes were visible when he smirked.

"Had fun learning languages from these tourists, I'm sure."

He laughed. "How about you?"

"I didn't grow up on an island."

"Cryptic," he mimicked her, and she laughed.

"Nah, I hardly ever ditched school. That was my brother's department. I was busy excelling at everything. Was your brother difficult, too?"

Niko just smiled, his gaze on the foaming water.

The smell of the beach, the noise, the warm sand, it was all there, but what Olivia felt the most was the touch of his hand against hers, their arms brushing as they strolled. Strangely, it was easier to imagine a fling with him when she had known him less. She wouldn't be able to bring herself to kiss him now, as she had before, and not because she didn't want to. In fact, she craved to.

At some point, leaving their shoes on the sand, outside the gentle waves reach, they stopped and looked at the clusters of people inside the water— children playing, two girls squealing and jumping into the sparkling crystal off the shoulders of their boyfriends. Niko bent and washed his hands and face in the salty water. Olivia did, too, then loosened what was left of her bun and brushed wet fingers through her hair. She had sat at the beach bar in front of him, her hair's a mess after the car ride, and hadn't even noticed.

When she shifted her gaze to Niko, she found him looking at her. "What?"

"Nothing." He smiled, then looked away.

"It's getting really hot," she said. "Should we go back?" The sun slanted toward the west, but it was still scorching. It wasn't the heat that made her say that, though. At least, not the heat of the sun.

The car was parked not far from a beach gear shop. When they reached it, Niko went inside the shop. Olivia remained on the sidewalk, baffled, in a forest of inflatable mattresses, pool noodles, hanging sets of sand toys, and a blinding selection of T-shirts and beach towels.

A moment later, Niko reappeared. "You're getting sunburned." He handed her a bottle of sunscreen.

Surprised, she took it from him. "Thanks!" she said after a beat.

He just winked a *don't mention it*.

After buckling up next to him, she rubbed sunscreen over her bare arms and shoulders.

"Roof off?" Niko asked, starting the engine.

"Yes, please."

"Then put some on your face, too." He smiled. "You have freckles."

She automatically raised her hand to touch the bridge of her nose.

"Do you want some?" She tilted the bottle toward him.

"Freckles?" Something in his smile and eyes made her breaths quicker. He then put his sunglasses back on and gestured toward the bottle. "No, thanks, already did at home."

Except for commentary on the emerald views, colorful beaches, and villages they drove past, they didn't speak much on the way back.

Niko parked the car in the alley behind the taverna thirty minutes later. As the roof slid back to its place, he removed his sunglasses, and his honey-green gaze met hers.

"I'll go in and see if Elena needs help," Olivia said hoarsely. She took her eyeglasses off and wiped them with the hem of her dress.

"You have"—Niko reached out and brushed his thumb across her right eyebrow—"sunscreen. Here, too." He smoothed his thumb slowly along her hairline.

"Thanks," she whispered.

With the roof on and the silence enveloping them, it felt like they were alone in the world.

With his fingers, Niko slowly caressed the loosened strands of her hair. Her breaths shallowed, and she dropped her gaze to his lips. Olivia inched a centimeter closer and that was all it took for Niko to lean in and close his lips on hers.

Chapter 10

Olivia brought her hands up, splaying her fingers over Niko's jawline and neck, fusing him to her. She drowned in that kiss.

Between breaths, she managed to whisper, slightly tilting her head in the general direction of the taverna. "Do you have to go in?"

"No."

Gazes stroking, devouring, they kissed again.

"Ouch." Her thigh hit the stick shift when she tried to cling closer to Niko's body.

"Do you want to come up?" Niko rasped.

"Yes."

He kissed her again and removed one of his hands from her. Then she heard the driver's door being opened. Reluctantly, they broke the kiss and climbed out of the car.

She followed him to a door that she had noticed before at the back of the building, to the right of the back entrance of the taverna. She didn't dare look around, as if she wouldn't see anyone, no one would see her.

They entered a tiny lobby with two mailboxes on the wall and a staircase. Climbing the stairs behind Niko, the noise from the taverna sounded like a steady hum, except for the music's bass pulsation that echoed that of her heart.

She followed him into the apartment and, as he turned to close the door, Niko's chest met hers. He placed his palms on her arms and grazed them up to her shoulders and neck without taking his eyes off her. Just like when they had kissed in the storage room, he released the scrunchie that tied her windswept hair and weaved his fingers into her mane. He then inclined his head and closed his mouth on hers more forcefully than before.

Olivia's body took the lead. Her mind didn't stand a chance. Her hands landed on his shoulders, and she trekked her palms over the broad expanse and down to smooth over his chest and back, clinging to the heat that his skin radiated through the fabric of his shirt.

When Niko kissed her neck, she opened her eyes and, through the haze, noticed the front door was still open. She reached out to shut it.

Niko slid his hands down her body, closed them around her thighs under the dress, and lifted her. She wrapped her legs around him and, somewhere in her hazy mind, Olivia hoped she wasn't heavy. But Niko soon made her oblivious again as he continued to kiss her while treading toward a bedroom.

She wanted all of her to touch all of him, with nothing to divide them, so Olivia pulled his shirt up and helped him take it off as soon as Niko placed her on the bed and came to lie on top of her.

On his shoulder, where she couldn't have noticed it before, was a tattoo. Why the discovery of it made her exhale in surprise, Olivia didn't know. Maybe because it was another layer, a sexy as hell one, to Niko, the former diplomat, that she hadn't expected to find. She brushed her fingers over it. A globe made of the continents in black ink with one area marked in pale aqua, and in it, a green dot. She didn't have to ask. It was the Adriatic Sea and a green island, his island.

She cupped his face and brought her mouth to his.

Soon, every piece of garment was discarded and flung to the floor. Everything inside her funneled to the nerve endings that touched Niko or were touched by him.

He was the first man she had been with since Jeff, but right now, after ten years, Olivia couldn't remember how Jeff felt or even looked. All she saw was the honey-green eyes looking at her, heavy-lidded, as she raked her fingers through the wavy, dark hair, the tan skin over the bare, taut body. In certain moments of lucidity, she heard her own huffed breaths intermixing with Niko's. All she felt was Niko's body hard and warm against hers, his caressing hands, his disarming mouth.

He sank deep inside her in more sense than one. The need in her increased with his every movement and touch to unbearable levels that could end only in detonation.

If Daria had unintentionally broadcasted to the world that Olivia hadn't enjoyed a decent orgasm in years, Olivia hoped that she herself wasn't broadcasting to the village that she was having one right there and then. She bit her bottom lip, but that didn't stop the moans that emanated from her throat, neither did Niko's kisses drown them.

Still panting in his arms later, Olivia felt the thumping of Niko's heart as she rested her head on his chest. When her breathing and heart rate steadied, she became aware again of the beat of the music from the taverna below that pulsated in the dusk-lit bedroom.

Giving in to the sweet heaviness of her limbs, she only moved her fingers across Niko's broad chest, sometimes trailing the plume of hair that descended to his abdomen. Niko's arm was wrapped around her, and he was raking his fingers through her hair.

"Won't they miss you down there?" she asked after a while. The words came out somewhat slurry.

"I don't work every day. Last Friday, I didn't, remember? I drove you to Corfu Town."

Last week, she had offered him to come into the house with her.

"It's surreal."

"What is?" Niko's lips were on her hair.

"That it's been a week. It feels longer, or shorter sometimes, but it doesn't feel like a week."

"I know the feeling." After a short pause, he added, "What parts of it feel longer or shorter to you?"

"Thinking about it, everything seems both longer and shorter—the days since I left Seattle, the conference, coming here, the house, the taverna." *Knowing you*, she wanted to add but didn't.

"What exactly happened to you at that conference?" Niko's voice rasped under her.

He had never pried before, always leaving her to decide how much she wanted to share. Using technology, he could have easily found out, and she appreciated he hadn't engaged in it.

Olivia hesitated, then slithered out of his arms and reached for her phone, which had been dropped absentmindedly on the nightstand before. She googled the humiliating hashtag, then handed the phone over to Niko, who had been looking at her the whole time.

"What is it?" he asked.

She sat up, covered in the comforter, and gestured with her head for him to go ahead and open it.

Niko tapped one of the search results.

Holding her breath, Olivia witnessed his expressions change as he watched the video—his jaw muscle twitched, his brows furrowed. She wasn't sure what had driven her to share this with him now, especially as it meant he had read everything in Daria's message to her. *Everything.* She was hiding, waiting for this thing to evaporate from everyone's minds, yet here she was, sharing it. But this was Niko, and while he could read everything, he wasn't everyone.

When the ninety-second video, which had felt like ninety minutes, was over, Niko raised his eyes from the screen to look at her. Then he dropped her phone between the pillows, reached toward her, and silently took her in his arms. He enveloped her, and she rested her cheek on his shoulder.

"I'm so sorry," he said after a while.

In a few sentences, she caught him up to how she had arrived late, bought that T-shirt, prepared as much as she could despite all the setbacks, and how her laptop had failed her.

"I can't believe you lost your job because of *that*. The people who filmed it and shared it should lose their jobs, not you."

"No one knows who they are, and no one wants to risk losing customers to find out."

"I'm sorry I pretended to not know English when you came in that day." He squeezed her tighter against him.

"Water under the bridge." Olivia chuckled. "But, you see, instead of my lecture on a meaningful project, this is what I'll be remembered for."

"It does have a memorable effect." He didn't sugarcoat it, but his intonation tried to make light of it, for her sake.

"Yes, it paints a vivid picture."

"If you can joke about it, it means that the worst is behind you."

Olivia rose to lean on her elbow and look at him again. He had just read about her sex life with Jeff and Daria's suggestions for improvement. He could have thrown a crude hint just now about getting under a hot Greek guy, but all he radiated was empathy.

"I can joke about it only because I'm far from everyone and everything that's related to it. Thanks for letting me stay here and be … a part of things." She skimmed her eyes over his face and bent to kiss him.

"Is this part of the volunteer work?" he rasped against her lips.

She laughed into his mouth, then deepened their kiss.

The only indication of the hour was when the music below ceased and a loud goodbye from one of the last customers was heard from the street.

"Kostas and Angie are closing," Niko commented.

They were in his kitchen, hovering together over containers of leftovers that Niko had reheated in a microwave.

"It's not very fresh anymore. I didn't have time to get a new supply from Elena today," Niko apologized. He was shirtless and in a pair of short cargo pants.

In a blue T-shirt that she had found thrown on the bed that was long enough to cover her panties, Olivia forked dolmades. "As you can see, I manage." She grinned.

The kitchen was connected to the living room and, straight ahead, they could see the large balcony. It overlooked the street below and the alleys behind it. Olivia was certain that, in daylight, the sea was also discernible. She didn't peek through the balcony, wordlessly agreeing with Niko that they shouldn't approach it lest they would be seen from the street.

The apartment looked like it belonged to a single man. It was plainly and functionally decorated. His suitcase still stood near the entrance and was the only evidence of the fact that he had been away and had only come back earlier that day.

Olivia pointed her fork at the luggage. "So, once a month, you fly to Athens?"

"Sometimes I drive there."

"To visit your brother and sister?" She picked inside a rice-stuffed sweet pepper.

"Yes."

For some reason, his monosyllabic reply made her raise her eyes and look at him. Their gazes met. "It's just that Nina said you have a sister and a brother there."

Niko smiled. "Nina is the family's narrator." He breathed in. "But yes, I have a brother and sister there. Andreas and Cleo."

"Am I asking too many questions?"

Niko chuckled through his, "No." Then, with a serious expression, he added, "Cleo's husband works there, so they moved there after they got married. They have two kids." He grazed his lower lip with his teeth. "And Andreas … we moved him there after our parents' accident."

Olivia's heart realized what she had heard before her mind did, and it jumped to her throat. "Moved him there?"

"Oh, *that* Nina didn't tell you?" He smiled again, but the crease lines around his eyes that usually adorned his smile weren't there.

She swallowed. "Tell me what?"

"Andreas lives in an assisted living facility for adults. He … there was a complication in his birth." He must have seen the shocked grimace on her face, because he then added with a smile, "Sorry you asked?"

"No. I'm just … I'm sorry to hear this."

"Don't' be. Cleo and I were born into this; that's how we've always known Andreas and loved him." Her expression must have prompted him to blurt it all out once and be done with it, because he then said, "It was harder on my parents, but he was doing well until *that* happened. Long story short, I took a leave of absence and remodeled their house so it'd be more comfortable for him—he's in a wheelchair. But, after a while, he didn't want to live there anymore. He wanted to try something different. Cleo found that place in Athens, so ..." Niko made a *nothing left to do* gesture by shrugging and turning his palms up. "He's happier there now."

Things fell into place. The spacious plan of the house, the doorframes that seemed wider than usual, the unused ramp that her foot had hit when she had been watering the plants the first time.

"Is that why you came back?" This was the last piece of the puzzle.

"No. I told you why I came back. Because, despite everything, people were happier here than I had been abroad. And, when I was here, I was happier, too."

There was a moment's silence, then Niko added, "Anyway, Andreas needed a few check-ups in hospital, nothing alarming, but Cleo couldn't be with him, so I had to fly there on Tuesday. Now you know everything."

Olivia put down the fork that hadn't been used since Niko had started his tale, circled the breakfast bar, and hugged him. With him sitting on a counter stool and her standing, they were at eye level. She buried her face in his neck and inhaled his skin.

A knock on his front door made them both freeze.

"It's Kostas." Niko was the first to recover.

"I'll go to the bedroom," Olivia whispered.

Through the open bedroom door, she could hear Niko speaking to his uncle. Being nearly caught half-dressed prompted Olivia to put her dress and shoes back on. The illusion of being just them had been broken.

When Niko entered the bedroom soon after, she was fully dressed, her eyeglasses on, and her hair carefully tied back.

"Sorry about that. He saw my car outside and the lights on here, so he brought me the check that the bride's father from Sunday dropped off."

"I should be going, anyway."

"You can stay."

"I don't think it's a good idea with you living right above the taverna." She wasn't sure why she cared if anyone knew about this. Maybe she'd had enough of her private life paraded publicly.

"I'll walk you." He didn't wait for a response, grabbing a shirt from an armchair that sat by the window.

"From your apartment to your house, sneaking by your taverna. Anything else you own in this village?" She swept her eyes over his naked torso.

Niko huffed a chuckle. "Nothing else."

The taverna below was dark and silent when they passed by it. Olivia had never seen it closed before. The streets were deserted.

At the house door, she turned to Niko. "Will you come inside?"

"If you're sure."

"It's your house." She fisted his shirt and pulled him in for a kiss.

As soon as they were in, Niko untied her hair again and slipped his fingers into her tousled curls without detaching his mouth from hers. He pushed the front door closed with his foot, lifted Olivia in his arms, and carried her to the bedroom.

Chapter 11

Dazzling sunlight filled the room and hit Olivia's closed lids like a bucket of cold water. She sat up and squinted. Her limbs felt heavy, her head a little dazed. Only when she was awake enough to realize she was naked under the white sheet did memories of the night dawned on her. She fell back on the pillow and smiled at the bright ceiling.

Is this what they teach in these little villages, or did Niko learn this abroad? Her body felt like it had been to the amusement park and had gone on all the best rides.

Showering then dressing in her new black pants and aqua blouse, images of the night before flashed in Olivia's mind. Niko kissing his way down her body, Niko whispering something in his language into her ear when he was inside of her. Niko's arm wrapped around her as she dozed into sleep.

When did he leave? The front door was locked, but her key rested on the console.

She went into the kitchen to make herself a cup of coffee. Under the coffee jar was a handwritten note.

"Good morning. See you for breakfast or lunch at the taverna. Niko." He had signed his name in Greek letters.

Olivia found herself grinning and pressing the note to her chest. Realizing it, she dropped it back onto the counter and pressed the electric kettle's button. She wasn't a teenager, and she couldn't allow herself to forget that her stay here was temporary.

On the short way to the main street, every set of eyes that met hers made Olivia self-conscious, as if the whole village had heard her the night before and knew exactly where she had been and what she had done.

At the taverna, Niko stood with his back to her, arranging bottles that he took out of crates and wearing different clothes than the ones she had taken off him last night.

She leaned against the bar. "Is it still *kalimera* or should I say *kalispera*?"

Niko turned. "You know it's still *kalimera*." He smirked. "Sleep well?" he added, and only the way he held her gaze hinted at what stood behind the question.

"Very well. You?"

"Great. I had to be here early, though."

Olivia canvassed the room. Besides the two tables of the regular forenoon coffee drinkers and backgammon players outside, there was no one around.

"I better go see what Elena needs before lunchtime." She didn't want to go, but it was awkward seeing Niko in the light of day and having to conceal the crave to put her hands on him and inhale his neck over the collar of that shirt. She was afraid the others would notice, that *he* would notice. Even now, the way he looked at her—pinning her with his gaze, and his lips wearing a playful smile— made her palms sweat.

Whether it was preparing HR guidelines, coaching managers, deploying programs, or waiting on tables, Olivia knew how to submerge herself in work so that hours could fly by before she had time to think. At the Teresi taverna, it was a bit harder. Niko was there whenever she approached the bar, went to bring Elena something from the back, or caught a glimpse of him chatting and joking in Greek with the regulars.

Things slowed down after three, and Olivia headed toward the bar to give Niko the payment of a table outside when Nina came in.

When they saw each other, the two women hugged as if they had known one another for years and had been separated for years.

Niko poured three glasses of fresh lemonade and signaled them to sit on the bar stools.

"I came to take my mother to the dentist," Nina explained in English. "My mother said you're doing a great job." She turned to Olivia. "I just can't believe you're still working. I'm glad you are—don't get me wrong. Niko told us that you wanted a quiet place to start learning about the hospitality industry. But you should use your time and have fun, too."

Olivia bit her upper lip and inhaled to stop herself from bursting into laughter. Her glance crossed paths with that of Niko's, who widened his eyes and inclined his head in Nina's direction, hinting that Olivia should play along. She appreciated that he had found a way to explain her presence without disclosing the embarrassing circumstances that had brought her here.

"I told Olivia she should come back to Corfu one day to get a better experience of it," he chimed in.

Olivia had to resist smirking this time. He had no idea that it would be hard, extremely hard, to exceed the experience that she'd had in Corfu last night. In her one week here, she had experienced two extremes—one of the most awful moments of her life and one of the best. She hoped the blush that spread on her face didn't reveal her thoughts.

"I took a little tour on Tuesday and, yesterday, Niko took me to Sidari."

"You took her to *Theia* Katerina?" Nina asked, looking at Niko.

"Yes, and to the beach there to have a drink," he replied.

Nina looked between them. She then got up and shouldered her purse. "Olivia, do you want to come with me and my family to the beach on Sunday? We go to a little cove that only locals know about. What do you say? Niko, come, too."

"That's the bonus in not having too many tourists—I can close, or open, whenever I want on Sundays," Niko said, looking at Olivia.

"I'll be happy to go," Olivia said. "Thanks, Nina."

She saw Nina to the kitchen where Elena was just hanging her apron on the hook rack. Olivia wondered if anyone had detected her name scribbled on the staff picture that hung next to it.

When Elena noticed them, she took out an envelope from her purse and handed it to Olivia.

Olivia automatically reached for it, but then she pulled back. "What is this?" she asked.

"Take, take, it's yours," Elena said, extending her arm even more.

"It's your share of the tips," Nina explained.

"Oh. No, thank you, Elena. Please, share it between you and Althea."

Elena just shook her head and kept her hand extended.

Nina took the envelope from her mother and held it against Olivia's chest. "She'll never agree to this. Take it. Besides, you earned it."

"I'm doing this for ..." She didn't want to say *for fun* or *to bide my time because I don't want to go home.* "... for learning," she ended up saying, remembering how Niko had explained her presence.

Neither woman spoke; they just stared at her, and Nina still held the envelope against her chest.

"Okay. Thank you. I appreciate this." Olivia took the envelope and smiled at Elena.

Nina leaned in and exchanged two kisses on the cheek with her. "No use arguing with my mother. Just ask Niko," she half-whispered, chuckling.

Althea arrived after the two had left, and Olivia tried to give her the envelope.

The girl shook her head. "Nina called to tell me you will try this."

"Your women folk insist I get a share of the weekly tips," Olivia informed Niko later. He was alone at the bar and, like a magnet, Olivia couldn't resist the pull and went there.

"I know. Elena updated me this morning, and I agreed with her. You can't work without getting paid. At least the tips."

"You know that you're practicing what I've been teaching managers for years?"

"What? Paying salaries?"

"No. Treating employees like you treat pretty much everyone."

"It's family," Niko said matter-of-factly.

"I'm not family." Her gaze was glued to his.

"You're not," he rasped.

And somehow, the way they held each other's gaze added a whole different layer to the words they uttered.

"I have to work late today," he said, confirming that the same thought had crossed their minds.

"You said Fridays were busy. I thought to go now and return later to help."

"Only if you want."

When she left the taverna for the house, Olivia wasn't sure if that had been a silent agreement that they would meet before the evening pressure began.

The answer wasn't late to arrive when Niko knocked on the house door fifteen minutes after she had entered it.

"Hi," was all they both managed to say before Niko took a step forward and they launched themselves at each other.

~~~~~~~~~~~~~~~~~~~~~~~~~~~~

Sometime later, Olivia, half-lying on Niko, leaned on her elbow, supported her head with her palm, and looked at him.

"Hi there," he said, grinning. He still had his fingers weaved through her hair, his palm nestling the back of her head, which made it easy for him to pull her into a lazy, satisfied kiss.

"Kostas replaced you?" she asked. They hadn't really spoken from the moment he had knocked on the door.

Niko signaled *yes* by blinking once.

"What did you tell him?"

"That I had to go and check on something."

"Oh, no."

"Why are you worried?"

"I'm not worried. I just … I don't know." Maybe making it public would make it too real, and with the way Niko made her feel, she couldn't afford it without irreversibly endangering her heart.

"No, I get it," Niko said. "I do have to get back, though." He raised himself from the bed. "Especially if you don't want him to suspect."

She could hear the amusement in his voice, though all she could see was his back. She enjoyed watching the muscles on his back roll as he put his shirt back on.

Sighing, Olivia got up, too. While she was getting dressed, her phone rang. The number on the screen was local. She tapped the green key and listened to the woman on the other end of the line.

"I can't believe this." She looked at Niko. "That was the airport. My suitcase arrived, and they sent it to the hotel, because that was the address I gave at the lost luggage counter. I can pick it up from the hotel. Is it okay if I go there tomorrow?"

"Of course it is." He approached her, fully dressed, and put his hands on her shoulders. "All my employees deserve time off," he teased.

~~~~~~~~~~~~~~~~~~~~~~~~~~~~~~~~~~~~~~

When Olivia returned to the taverna that evening, an hour after Niko had left the house, she wore her new, flowery dress. She was glad she had worn her sneakers with it because the taverna was full. More importantly, there was a large table of two families and friends who seemed to be celebrating something, judging by the number of ouzo rounds that had been served to their table.

At some point, three of the men pushed their chairs back, took out musical instruments that were hidden in cases on the floor next to them, and started playing. First, the rest of their party and, later, people from other tables jumped up, formed lines and circles, and created a spontaneous dance floor by pushing tables back to make room.

Darius, one of the regulars, a man in his late sixties with the soul of a sixteen-year-old, took Olivia's hand as she stood by, watching, and pulled her to join them.

Just when her throat was chafing with the exultation of dancing and laughing and calling "*Opa*" with the rest, a drink was shoved into her free hand. She looked up and saw Niko beaming at her.

"*Yamas*," he said.

He wasn't allowed to go back to the bar, and instead was drawn to join the dancing. Olivia had another opportunity to witness how confident, masculine, and sexy he was.

That night, after most of the people had left, Niko told Althea she could leave, too.

When it was just him and Olivia, he approached, slithering his arms around her waist from behind, and kissed her neck. He then spun her to face him, whispering, "Finally."

After he locked up, they barely made it fully clothed to his apartment.

Chapter 12

"Do you have your driving license with you, or is it in the suitcase you're picking up?" Niko asked when they arrived at the house two hours later.

He had offered to escort her there when she had said she didn't want to be seen coming out of his apartment the morning after.

"I do. Why?"

"You can take my car to Corfu Town."

They had just reached her front door, and she leaned against it, facing him. "That is very, very generous of you," she muttered against his lips, pressed between him and the wooden surface. "But no, thank you. I don't want to be responsible for your poison-green car on unfamiliar roads. You seem very attached to it." She chuckled. "I'll take the bus."

"I have to be here tomorrow, or I'd drive you."

"You're doing more than enough without being my chauffeur."

"I can do a lot more than that," he mumbled into her neck.

~~~~~~~~~~~~~~~~~~~~~~~~~~~~~~

The road to Corfu Town, that reflected through the large windows of the bus, looked familiar now that it was the third time Olivia had seen it. She wasn't afraid to show up at the hotel now that the conference had ended but decided to spend the morning in town before taking a taxi to pick up her suitcase.

Walking the bustling streets of the city, Olivia regretted not wearing a dress, as it was too hot to be in jeans. That morning, she had felt she had a little more space inside her new jeans, which had been tighter when she had bought them as a counterreaction to the baggy flight pants. It might have been the Mediterranean food, the physical work, vigorous bedroom activity, lack of appetite in her first few days in Greece, or all of it combined, but she felt energetic and healthier than she had been in a while.

Her first stop was a hair salon. It was the one she remembered from strolling the city center with Niko a week before. She walked in and was lucky to find them able to accept her for a blowout.

It was so familiar to sit in the chair, smell the products that would finally get her hair back under control, and hear the chatter of the employees and customers. Although she couldn't understand a word of it, it sounded like the chats that were held in every hair salon on the planet. Most satisfying of all was watching through the mirror how her hair slowly got that orderly, perfected look.

Half of her hair still looked like it wanted to escape her head—"You should do something with all that hair," she remembered Jeff's words—while the other half sat obediently on her shoulder when an email pinged on her cell phone.

Olivia opened it, trying not to get in the way of the woman who was working on restraining her curls.

"We are happy to announce that your work on "Mix With Caution: Familial Concepts In The Workplace" was elected to be presented at our HR4Excellnce summit in San Jose, CA, on July 1st," the first lines announced.

Olivia read the details with a beating heart.

At the very end of the email, a personal note was added.

> *Dear Ms. Duncan,*
>
> *We are well-aware of the recent mishap at the HR Meets Engineering conference and were abhorred by the treatment you had received from fellow professionals. We'll be more than happy to have you present your project at the summit's opening ceremony. If using the name of your previous employer and customer is prohibited, you can talk about the principles of your work without using brand names.*
>
> *On behalf of the organizing team,*
> *Lynn Michaels.*

Olivia's hand shot up by itself to cover her mouth.

"Everything is okay?" the pretty lady who was doing her hair asked. "I pull too hard?"

"No, no, it's not you. I just received very good news."

"Congratulations. Your hair will be pretty for the good news."

"Yes, it will. Thank you." Olivia smiled at the woman through the mirror. She then forwarded the email to Daria. She had to share it with someone.

Though it was a small town, it was big enough for Olivia to breathe in a city atmosphere again. She enjoyed recognizing her reflection in the shops' windows and strove not to think about the date in July that had been indicated in the otherwise encouraging email.

The cab driver waited outside while she went into the hotel lobby to repossess her suitcase. In five minutes, she was wheeling it behind her toward the car's trunk.

Could this day get any better? Her hair was impeccable, she had her clothes, makeup kit, and contact lenses, and she wasn't completely ruined professionally.

It was late in the afternoon when Olivia disembarked the bus at Aleniki's main square. It looked so quaint in comparison to the bustle that she had come from. She had to overcome the urge to go straight into the taverna and parade her new old-self and tell Niko her good news.

Strangely excited, given that it was her own suitcase, Olivia unzipped it, hoping to find her treasures intact. The suit she had prepared for her lecture lay on top of everything and wasn't too wrinkled. She smoothed her hand over its creases, then unpacked everything, glad to be reunited with her button blouses, slacks, and high heels.

Standing in front of the bedroom's full-length mirror in her dark grey pencil skirt that reached just to her knees, a pearl-white top under the jacket and matching high heels, with full makeup and no glasses, Olivia wished that this was how Niko had first seen her instead of the wet cat version that had walked into his taverna. Well, it wasn't too late.

Armored in her outfit, Olivia marched the village curvy alleys, releasing her heels from between the pebbled surface whenever they got stuck. She noticed the looks thrown at her by the few locals who crossed her path.

Swiping a hand over her flattened hair, then straightening her jacket, Olivia entered the taverna.

The place was half full at this hour of the evening, and she nodded to a few people at the tables outside. Althea was serving two tables inside, but Olivia darted her gaze toward the bar. Niko, handsome as ever, in a button-down white shirt folded to his elbows, with the top two buttons open, was leaning his forearms on the bar, deep in conversation.

Olivia's stomach plummeted. She could only see the back of the trim figure that sat on a bar stool in front of him. The long hair waved down an off-shoulder, white top, and the boho skirt flowed off the chair. Thalia, fresh from her art and yoga retreat in Mykonos.

From the table right by the entrance, Darius stopped her and said something in broken English about how pretty she looked. Olivia listened halfheartedly because, just then, she saw Niko extracting something from his jeans pocket and handing it over to Thalia. When Thalia took it from him, Olivia could see the metallic glint of keys.

Something about it reminded her that they had known each other forever and shared nationality, language, culture, community, and even a bed once. She was a stranger among them.

An instinct commanded her to turn around and leave, but she ignored it and walked in. The pencil skirt limited her stride, and her heels clanked hollowly on the terracotta floor, despite her effort to subdue the sound. She smoothed a hand over her straight hair again.

Niko must have seen her in his periphery because he briefly glanced toward her approaching figure before returning his gaze to Thalia.

He didn't recognize her.

At that moment, in the taverna where she had known herself to be one thing, Olivia hardly recognized herself, either.

When she was near enough and Niko raised his eyes again and observed who she was, the expression that flashed across his face right before he straightened up reminded her of his reaction to her "*I heart Greece*" shirt.

"Olivia, hi. You got your suitcase," Niko said, as if pointing out the culprit. "You look nice. And …" He didn't say the word, just pointed toward her hair.

She caught a strand and smoothed it between her fingers. "Yes. This is how I usually style it … back home."

"And no glasses," he commented, pointing at his own eyes absentmindedly. It was as if he was taking stock of everything that had changed in her.

Thalia pivoted on the bar stool. Her face was tan and clean of makeup. "Oh, hi, Olivia," she said, her gaze scrutinizing Olivia from her pumps to her frizz-less hair. "I like your suit."

"Thanks," she replied. Although Thalia seemed sincere, Olivia wondered what she really thought of her last year's discounted designer suit persona.

"Sit with us," Niko said. "Do you want something to drink?"

More than anything, it was the semi-formality, the *us*, that sent a sudden twinge to Olivia's heart.

She took a seat next to Thalia, realizing that, to any bystander, of the two of them, Thalia looked like the woman who most likely had spent the previous night in Niko's bed, the woman who would suit him, and not the woman in the suit.

"Rakomelo, please," she said, needing the warmth of the honey drink.

"So, how was Corfu Town?" Thalia asked. She was obviously up to date with Olivia's business, and Olivia wondered if she also knew about her and Niko.

"It was good. I walked around a bit. Lots of people."

"Yes. Also in Mykonos and Neo Limani. That's why I love coming here to relax." The village she had named was the one next to Aleniki, where Olivia had bought clothes on her first day.

"You live there?" Olivia asked.

Niko placed a drink on the counter, then turned to talk to Althea, who had just approached the bar with an order.

"My studio is there. I also sell in a gallery in Corfu Town. You might have passed by it today. I have to be where the buyers are, and tourists are a good business."

"Tell Niko that," Olivia joked. He had just returned to his place, facing them.

"Oh, he knows." Thalia chuckled.

"That tourists are a good business?" he immediately picked up.

"I like that Aleniki is the way it is. I'm the only tourist here."

"We don't consider you a tourist anymore," Niko said. The smile on his face was warm, and he finally felt like the man who had caressed and kissed every inch of her the night before.

"Thank you." Their gazes locked. But his words brought back the fact that she had news to share that meant the hourglass of her stay had been turned. For a brief second after receiving the email, she had been glad that her professional achievements would be recognized and subconsciously avoided the fly in the ointment—having to attend the summit opening in less than two weeks. She had known Niko for about the same duration.

Time had never seemed more relative to Olivia.

"When are you due back home?" Thalia asked.

Is she a mind reader? Olivia wondered.

"Well, I received some news today," she opened, looking at Niko. "I was invited to present my project in a Human Resources awards ceremony." Olivia gazed into Niko's eyes, knowing he would understand the significance of this. She hoped Thalia wasn't enough in the loop to understand it, as well.

Niko pursed his lips and nodded in appreciation. "Wow. That *is* good news. When is this happening?"

"Oh, um, the ceremony is on July first." She hoped he didn't notice the catch in her voice.

Niko just nodded again, breaking eye contact. "Congratulations."

"Congratulations," Thalia echoed. "You're training for it with the suit?"

Olivia snickered. "You can say that. I was supposed to wear it to present at a conference here," Olivia wondered again if Thalia knew about the conference. "When I opened my suitcase today, I couldn't resist." She hoped this would explain to Niko, too, why she was overdressed, but Niko wasn't looking at her.

"You remind me of Niko when he first returned," Thalia said. "Suits and diplomatic language."

This brought his confession about him and Thalia vividly into Olivia's mind.

"How was your workshop?" she asked to block it from her mind.

"Oh, it was great. I was just telling Niko that there were …" She went on to share a few anecdotes about the participants, but Olivia only heard it as background noise. She was busy watching Niko, who moved aside to pour drinks and wipe the countertop.

"Oh no," Olivia commented, managing to catch Thalia's latest sentence about a couple who had tried to convince her to do a nude yoga session.

"Nina stopped by earlier to ask if you're going to the beach with them tomorrow," Niko turned to Olivia a few moments later.

"Oh. I almost forgot about it," she said, reflexively raising her hand to touch her hair. She had hoped to keep it intact at least one more day. "Will you go, too?"

"I don't know. I have a few things—"

"If they go to Liapades, you shouldn't miss it, Olivia. It's beautiful there," Thalia said. "I'd join you, but I have to be at the studio tomorrow."

"Are you open tomorrow?" Olivia directed her eyes at Niko right after nodding quickly and smiling to acknowledge Thalia's words. "If you are, I'll help."

"No, no, you go with Nina. I'll join if I can."

Olivia hoped that Thalia would hurry to say goodbye as she had done the two times that she had met her before, but Thalia lingered, and they maintained a fragmented chitchat about the views and places that Olivia had seen and about the difference between the Ionian islands that Corfu belonged to and the Cyclades islands that Mykonos was a part of. All that time, Niko busied himself with the bar, the storage room, or chatted with a few people who had stopped by on their way out.

Something was different about him. He exuded tension, but she couldn't point her finger as to the reason. Was it her and her news? Was he feeling uncomfortable with her and Thalia sitting there together? Were those keys that he had given Thalia back the reason? Was Thalia waiting for her to leave as much as she was waiting for Thalia to leave?

Olivia felt suffocated in the suit and high heels. After another half an hour of forced conversation, followed by long moments of silence when she and Thalia had run out of things to say, Olivia decided to leave.

There were still patrons who didn't seem in a hurry to go home. Maybe Niko would come over to the house after he closed up.

~~~~~~~~~~~~~~~~~~~~~~~~~~~~~~~~~~

Except for the bedroom when Niko had been there with her, Olivia's favorite part of the little house was the veranda. Sitting on the chair and playing quiet music through her phone, she hoped to hear his knock on the door. In the meantime, she struggled to convince herself that she wasn't jealous of Thalia. Most probably, what Thalia had shared with Niko was what she herself shared with him— friendship and sex. The main difference was that she hadn't known Niko for long and wasn't rooted here like him or Thalia.

Instead of a knock, her phone buzzed, startling her just when she was reaching the logical conclusion that there surely couldn't be deep or real feelings or potential for a future between herself and Niko, anyway. Logic had nothing to do with the way her heart sank when Daria's name flashed on the screen instead of his name.

"*Any chance you're up?*"

"*Yep. Call me,*" she texted back.

"Babes, I have amazing news for you!" Daria opened with the moment Olivia picked up. "As soon as I saw that email you sent me, I forwarded it to Kaylin. Remember her? My friend at Uno? I haven't had a chance to tell you yet, but they want to interview you for a senior HRBP role. I know it's Saturday, but I called her. She said the interview is just a formality, anyway, and that, with this email, there's no doubt they'll want to sign you up. Isn't this amazing?"

"Yes, amazing. Thank you," Olivia half-mumbled. She knew she should feel more excited about it. In fact, she should be ecstatic. Uno was a great company that Teamtastic had been trying to land as a customer for years, and the HR Business Partner role was pretty much a dream. It must be the shock. Too much good news for one day.

"I know, right? You see? I told you everything would turn out for the best. Now, spill. How are you doing there? *Who* are you doing there?"

Olivia laughed halfheartedly.

"I know something's going on. Got under a hot guy?"

Olivia took a deep breath. "Let's just say that you can mark a check on all the points you wrote in your message that everyone read."

"Damn! So, got under a hot Greek guy—check. Noteworthy orgasms—check. And he went down there? That's my girl! I want details. But not right now. Believe it or not, I'm at my parents' for lunch. When are you coming back? Your presentation is in less than two weeks."

Olivia swallowed a sigh. "I know. I have to think about it."

"What's to think about? You're doing this, right?"

"No. Yes. I'm coming back. I just … have to plan, that's all."

There was background noise on Daria's side, and then Olivia could hear Daria's mother's voice.

"My mom sends her regards and says I should join you." Daria chuckled.

"Now, *that* would be amazing!"

"Hell yes! Anyway, I have to go back inside. We're eating."

"Tell your parents hi from me. Kisses. Bye."

Alone in front of the vast, dark view, with the distant lights twinkling all around her, Olivia thought that, if she could move everything and everyone here, it would be perfect. But that was impossible, and things back home were lining up for her. She couldn't lose sight of the path. Hadn't she committed to it herself and invested years in it? She thought she had lost it just over a week ago, and now things were looking up again.

So, why wasn't she more excited? Why did getting back to her life seem like a sacrifice? And why was she yearning for Niko so much it hurt? She knew it wasn't just about what her body had discovered in the last seventy-two hours, because it couldn't explain the tug in her heart. It couldn't explain how something inside her had wilted and rebelled at the thought of going away and maybe never seeing him again.

Olivia wished she had answers to even half the questions that ping-ponged inside her head. She wished her heart would stop interfering as if it had all the answers.

Chapter 13

On the veranda again the next morning, Olivia took a selfie with the view so she would have something to send her mother. A wide smile accompanied her long-lost sunglasses and her new red swimsuit, along with a caption that said she was meeting with a friend named Nina to go to the beach. She had almost wished she didn't have Nina's phone number so she would have an excuse to reach out to Niko, but Nina had beaten her to it and had sent her a text message earlier that morning. She must have obtained Olivia's number from Niko. At least one of them had been in touch with him.

Since she hadn't packed for a vacation, Olivia had no proper beachwear. Reluctant to ruin one of her shirts or dresses, she put on the "*I heart Greece*" T-shirt and the pair of baggy jeans that she had landed with, folded to her knees. Fashion-challenged tourist or not, Olivia took a scrunchie to later tie her hair up tightly so it wouldn't get wet, and then she put on the sunscreen that Niko had bought her. She trailed her finger over the white cream on her eyebrow and at her hairline like he had done just a few days before.

To busy herself, she watered the plants and put her clothes in the washing machine that she had discovered in a shed at the side of the house on an earlier occasion. But changing beddings in the bedroom, vivid memories of her nights with Niko danced before her eyes. She held the pillow cover that Niko had slept on against her face and sniffed it deeply in. Traces of his aftershave made her stomach clench with an irresistible urge to drop everything and go to him. But she had no idea if the taverna was open or if he was at home. More importantly, she had no idea how *his* night had ended. So, she just waited for Nina, sitting on the front steps.

"*We took a bigger car. Meet us at the square*," a text message appeared five minutes later.

With a mix of excitement and nervousness, Olivia crossed the alleys to the main street. Her heart missed a beat. Observing from a distance, she saw that the taverna was open.

"*I can close, or open, whenever I want on Sundays*," she recalled Niko's words.

He was avoiding her.

A minivan was parked close to the village square and, through the open window, Nina waved at her to hurry.

"Sorry about the mess," Nina said, instructing Olivia with a hand gesture to get into the back.

As soon as Olivia was inside, Nina introduced her husband, Matteus, and reminded her of their kids' names—Adrian, who was seven, and Alexander, who was four.

"Your hair. I like it," Nina said, looking over her shoulder at Olivia.

"Thanks. I was in Corfu Town yesterday. My lost luggage finally arrived, so I took the chance and …" Olivia smiled and pointed at her hair.

During the ride, Olivia was too focused on the gorgeous views outside to notice the kids' beach gear poking the back of her head. Then they soon parked and carried everything toward a private nook on a sandy beach. There were only a few people around.

"It's busier in July," Nina explained.

After a few sentences exchanged with her husband in Greek, Nina deposited the children and their inflatable swim rings with Matteus and went into the water with Olivia.

"It's so good to have some quiet time with a friend," Nina said as soon as they were in.

The water was smooth as a mirror and as clear.

"Oh, my God, I needed that!" Olivia lowered herself into the water and swam around, trying hard to keep her hair from getting wet. It was rolled and tied into a bun at the top of her head.

"Do you have the sea where you live?" Nina asked.

"The ocean, yes, but it's nothing like this. It's very cold and not as clear and soothing."

"When are you going back?"

"Sometime soon." Olivia didn't feel like going into it, not because of Nina, but because she didn't want to think about it herself.

"The hospitality business is big. You are in Human Resources, right? You want to combine it?"

"I haven't thought about it much." Olivia realized she sounded rude and flaky, but she just wished she could submerge herself again in not thinking about the situation as she had done in her first week here. Now reality kept knocking, and she wasn't ready yet to open the door and admit it in.

"I'm sorry, Nina. I'm not trying to avoid answering. It's just that I haven't really planned anything. I should, though. It's very unlike me to not plan."

"If you want, I have a friend who works in a large hotel farther down from here, but it's still not too far from Aleniki. It belongs to an international chain. Maybe they're looking for workers."

They weren't far from the shore and could easily stand inside the water, waist-deep, and talk.

"I don't know if they'll want me. I specialized mostly in high-tech. And besides, I can't stay here."

"Why not?"

"Because … I'm not from here."

"You're right. But many people who live here are from England, for example. But I understand— family, friends, country. It's not easy to change. Only if you have something really big and important waiting for you at a new place."

Olivia turned to look at Nina. That last sentence sounded like a hint.

"Do you have something with Niko?" Nina asked, verifying Olivia's suspicion.

"Something?"

"I see how he looks at you."

"How?" Why were her stomach and heart clenching like that?

Nina broke eye contact and stared ahead, to where the cove's shoulders opened into the sea. "It's okay if you don't want to tell me, but I think you have something with him. I don't need to be there every day to see it. I saw it at the wedding, and I saw it on Friday. Even more on Friday. At first, I thought, *This is Niko, he always treats people well. It's in his blood.* I know you don't speak our language, but *philoxenia*, it's the hospitality, the respect for strangers."

Olivia huffed a little reminiscent chuckle. "You should have seen how he pretended to not know English when I first came into the taverna."

"Oh, maybe he thought you were just one of those tourists who badly use our *philoxenia*." Nina seemed to hesitate, which was unusual. "Do you know what killed his parents? Drunk tourists that came for a weekend, ruined their hotel room—this is what we found out later—and drove a rented car right into his parents' car when they were on their way to the bank."

"Oh, my God!" Olivia covered her mouth with a wet hand. "He never told me that. I wish you had told me sooner, Nina."

"No, it could only make you feel strange or bad. And I try not to gossip. My mother calls me *koutsompola*. It means like *gossip girl*, but it's not nice."

"I think you're very nice, Nina."

"Thank you. I think you're very nice, too. What I want to say is that Niko, he doesn't look at you like a guest or friend. He has a different feeling in his eyes. I don't think he had many girlfriends since he came back. He never tells me, but I know, like I know he has something with you. I saw a few with him. I remember one was from Athens and one who moved from England or Ireland or something like that."

Olivia shifted on her feet.

The movement drew Nina out of her stream of consciousness. "I'm sorry," she said. "I'm doing it again. I tell stories that people don't want to hear. What I did want to say, and I hope you don't mind, is that I never saw him looking at anyone like he looks at you. I don't know you enough, but I hope you feel he's special, too."

Olivia chewed on her lower lip. No, no, it wasn't hope that was raising its head inside her.

She was saved from replying by the entry of Matteus and the children into the water and the latter demanding their mother's attention.

If Niko felt for her and looked at her in a way his cousin had never seen on him before, why wasn't he there when he could have come? Why did he stay away from her last night and remained with Thalia? And what did it all matter, anyway, when she was just a visitor here?

~~~~~~~~~~~~~~~~~~~~~~~~~~~~~~~~~~

Two hours later, when they were getting ready to leave, one of the boys hollered at something behind them and bolted. Olivia and Nina, who were deflating the kids' swim rings, spun around.

Olivia's breath hitched.

Jumping into his cousin's arms and being raised to sit on his shoulders, the boy victoriously squealed and waved at them.

Niko, in sunglasses and a wide smile, his muscular chest showing even through the short-sleeved, white T-shirt, and in a pair of dark olive-green board shorts, approached them.

Nina could have detected all the answers she was looking for if she looked at Olivia at that moment. Olivia was certain it was written all over her.

Niko patted his cousin-in-law's back and carefully bent his head to kiss Nina on both cheeks, dropping a beach towel that he held on the sand next to her. All the while, the child, who had managed to snatch Niko's sunglasses, kept chattering happily on his shoulders.

Olivia stood beside Nina, and there was a visible halt in Niko's movement when he turned toward her.

He reached up, grabbed the child under his armpits, and lowered him to the sand. He then straightened up and locked eyes with Olivia's. For a moment, everything around them disappeared.

"Hi," he said. The intimacy he could convey with one word sent a pang to her lower belly and turned her knees to rubber.

"Hi," she replied.

Then, in a sudden attack, the boy's younger sibling launched himself at Niko and wrapped his arms around his leg. Niko swayed without removing his eyes from Olivia, then bent and picked him up, raising him high above his head until the four-year-old sat safely on his shoulders. The child kicked Niko's chest with his heels. Niko said something to him in Greek, then ran across the sand with his happy, squealing charge.

Olivia tried to refocus on helping Nina pack and felt the other woman's gaze boring a hole into her. Looking up, their gazes met.

Nina raised an eyebrow, then patted Olivia's arm twice with a mischievous smile.

Olivia scoffed. There was no way to conceal what had just transpired.

When Niko and the boy returned, Nina urged her family in Greek, then turned to Niko and said in English, "We are leaving, but you will drive Olivia back, okay?"

Olivia appreciated Nina's effort to make it seem casual.

And, as if Niko wanted to convey the same, he rubbed Nina's shoulder. "Sure."

Olivia and Niko, standing side by side, watched the family of four leave. Only when they disappeared behind the boulders that divided the sandy beach from the gravelly road that led to it, they turned to look at each other.

Niko raised his sunglasses to rest on the top of his head. He skimmed his eyes over Olivia's face. "Hi again," he rasped.

"Hey."

"I'm sorry I couldn't be here earlier."

"You're here now."

"Race you?" he called, already taking a step toward the water.

Olivia laughed and started after him. By the time she reached the water and was knee-high inside, Niko had already discarded his shirt and sunglasses on the beach and dived into the turquoise.

She managed to take a few more steps in when Niko reappeared, shaking his head and running both hands over his wet face and hair. He was gorgeous.

"Now you," he said, approaching her, slightly panting.

"I …" To say that she didn't want to wet her hair sounded ridiculous now, even inside her own head. - She was on a Greek island with a man who had seen her at her shabbiest and desired her, if the way he touched her could attest to that. More importantly, everything seemed to dwarf when those honey-green eyes focused on her. The blowout, the suit, the speech, even the promised job, it all seemed trivial. The only thing that mattered, the only thing she wanted to hold on to was this look on his face, that glint in his eyes.

What was happening to her?

She had never been much of a swimmer, but Olivia arched her body forward, extended her arms arrow-like, and took the plunge.

Her eyes stung, and her face and hair dripped, but reemerging out of the water to find Niko so close made it all worthwhile. He was waiting for her, waist-deep in the water. She took a step toward him and, even in the cool water, could feel the heat of his body radiating toward her. He reached out to her, and she stepped into his embrace, linking her arms behind his neck and connecting her body with his. Niko grazed his hands down her thighs and brought them up to wrap around him while crushing his mouth on hers.

That kiss tasted of Niko and salt, and if there hadn't been other people close by, Olivia would have happily peeled off the layers that separated them and felt him to the utmost. His body signaled to her that he was ready to do the same.

When they stopped to breathe, Niko smoothed his palms over her cheeks and wet hair. Like he had done before, he released the scrunchy and weaved his fingers into her hair, ruffling it until it curled around her face. "Much better," he rasped, then kissed her again.

They walked hand-in-hand to the sandy shore, picked up Niko's shirt, and spread their towels. Niko lay on his back, and she rested her head on his shoulder, feeling his heartbeat beneath her. It was strange how they fell into cadence with each other.

"I'm so glad you came." She trekked her fingers along the salty drops on his chest. "What happened yesterday?"

He didn't reply. Instead, he wrapped an arm around her.

"Is it about Thalia?" she dared.

"No."

She raised herself and looked at him. Her head and hair shaded his eyes, and he could return her gaze without much squinting.

"I missed you," she said. The truth of it overpowered her. Things between them had developed fast, and she didn't feel like she had missed him just yesterday or that morning, but longer than that, maybe even before she had known him.

As if another set of three words had dropped from her mouth, Olivia awaited his response, frightened at her own confession and what he would think of her.

"I missed you, too," he said, surveying her eyes with his own while toying with her curls.

Relief, as clear and soothing as the sea, washed Olivia's insides. She wanted to ask more but decided to wait. Instead, she laid her head on his shoulder again.

The sunrays caressed and dried their bodies, and a light breeze ensured it wouldn't become unbearably hot.

"I love this cove," Niko said. "It's perfect for *aragma*."

"What's that?"

"I think you would call it *chilling*. It's a state of mind, not just what you do."

She was never good at relaxing—her mind always raced—but Niko's presence enveloped and soothed her in a way she had only realized it did when it was gone. Like a rock absorbing the heat of the sun, he seemed to have been able to absorb her anxiety and embarrassment almost from the very beginning. Even now, she was pacified enough to practically feel the vitamin D soaking into her body, though another part of her was hyper-alert to Niko's proximity. Olivia wished she could hang on to this as her only reality and stop the sand from draining in the hourglass.

After going into the water again and kissing a lot more, Niko offered they go back to his apartment to eat.

"I'm starting to like this shirt, but only on you," he said, smiling playfully when he noticed the T-shirt she had put on. He ran a finger over the heart shape between the words *I* and *Greece.* "Yes, I think I'm going to love this shirt." He bent and kissed her again.

Food and shower had to wait until after they stumbled into his bedroom and satiated another kind of hunger, filling his sheets with whispers and sand.

"I want to sit outside and watch the sunset with you," Niko said later as they ate out of the plastic containers from the taverna. "Would my balcony be okay, or are you still hiding?"

"Not hiding, but the veranda is beautiful and doesn't face the street."

"Still hiding." He winked.

At the house, Niko dragged the deep and wide armchair from the living room and onto the veranda. There, Olivia curled up against him in it. The sunset on the island was something she thought everybody should see at least once in their lifetime.

"You asked about yesterday," he opened after a long moment, his voice gravelly in the silent, fragrant evening air.

"Yes." Olivia shifted against him as if she was trying to dig herself deeper into him.

"I don't know what happened. I was waiting for you to come back, and then, when you arrived, you looked so different. It's stupid. I'm sorry. You looked beautiful."

"No, it's not stupid. I felt it, too. At first, I was excited to have my things back, but then I felt like I was borrowing clothes from someone else. Now, *that's* stupid."

"No, it's still you. I think it just reminded me that you're leaving soon. It was stupid and selfish. "

Her heart stopped. Was Nina right?

"You don't want me to go?"

"No." Then, as an afterthought, he added, "Not yet, at least. Not unless you want to."

Olivia swallowed. "I don't want to go yet, either. I'm trying not to think about it."

"You have to think about it. You have that ceremony to attend. I know how important it is after what happened." He rubbed a hand over her arm and tightened his hold around her. "I was angry with myself, but we closed late, so I didn't want to wake you."

"I was hoping you'd come. I waited. I'm sorry I didn't tell you or call you myself. I thought it was because of Thalia."

"Why?"

"Tell me about her. What's your connection to her?"

"Thalia was Andreas's art therapist. The pictures over there"—he pointed in the direction of the living room—"are his and hers."

Olivia kept silent. It was another piece of the puzzle.

"She's very talented and became a good friend to the family long before I came back. I met her after the … tragedy with my parents, and there was the whole thing with Andreas, who wanted to move from a place he had known all his life. We had a lot of discussions and conversations and … something happened between us. But it was short and ended long ago. Nothing you should …"

"What?"

"I wanted to say nothing you should worry about, but I don't want to presume."

"I *did* worry about her, and I'm glad I don't have to. I was jealous. I mean, she could suit you so much better than me. She's from here and a family friend, sophisticated but also very … island-y."

"Yes, but Thalia, she never makes mistakes. You know those people who never make any mistake and they just flow?"

"I envy those people. I'm afraid of making mistakes."

"Well, something is not realistic about it, something fundamental is missing. I like people who make mistakes and deal with them, especially those who are afraid of making mistakes and still make them. People who wear ridiculous T-shirts and tell rude people what they think of them to their face, especially if they think the other person doesn't understand. I like people who think they don't know how to dance and dance, anyway; who don't know a language but sing it, anyway; people who think their hair needs to be perfect but ask to have the roof off in the car. Do you know such people?"

These aren't tears that are stinging the back of my throat, Olivia told herself.

"I think I do," she whispered.

Niko buried his face in her neck and, under her ear, whispered, "I like people who can wake the whole village up with the noise they make in bed. It's a big mistake. You know such people?"

Olivia's response didn't resemble intelligible words, because Niko nibbled on her earlobe and kissed her neck before he caught her lips and drowned that incoherent mumble in a deep, demanding kiss.

Chapter 14

Later that night, they drank wine, cuddled together again on the armchair, watching the moon light up the surface of the dark blue sea.

"*Can I call?*" her mother's message dinged loudly in the silent night.

"My mother is about to call," Olivia warned Niko.

Thirty seconds after she typed her reply, the phone rang. Olivia got up and went into the house.

"When are you coming back?" was her mother's first question after the initial greetings.

"Soon."

"When is *soon*? Do you have enough vacation days left? Because, if not, that's a long vacation with no salary," Accountant Becky Duncan said.

Pacing the kitchen floor back and forth, Olivia finally told her mother the truth. "It's not just a vacation, Mom. They fired me—Teamtastic. And before you say anything, I'm not going to fight for it or sue them. I'll find something else, and I'll find it soon. In fact, Daria already has something lined up for me." She stopped and rearranged the sugar and coffee containers that stood next to the electric kettle, letting her mother's cycle of shock, disdain, hope, and advice subside.

"Olivia, you just lost your job, and you sound too laid-back about this." *Laid-back* for her mother was the equivalent of the deadly sin, sloth.

"I'm getting severance pay. Please, don't worry. And please, don't talk to Maria Soltis, okay? Her son works in a very different field, and I already have something through Daria. Oh, and I almost forgot …" She went on to share the news about the presentation at the summit, in hope that this would soften the blow for her mother.

Effusions followed this update. "So, you have to get back before July first."

"I plan to." Uttering it out loud felt like she had just put an official time limit on her stay here.

"Plan to? Olivia, you gave yourself time. Now it's time to get back to reality. Don't lose the momentum. You have to be perfect at that summit so you can pick up from where you left off with that … Greece fiasco. If you act right, it'll be just a glitch and you can recourse. What are you doing there all this time, anyway?"

"I tour and … I help in a taverna in the village where I stay." The last part dropped from her mouth fast.

"Help in a taverna?" her mother echoed. There was a long pause in which Olivia could almost hear her mother forming sentences and thinking the better of it. Over a sigh, Becky then added, "Okay. If this is part of your vacation, then okay. Just make sure it's not—"

"Too much of a good thing. I know, Mom. Give Dad a hug for me."

If anything, this was too little of a good thing.

When she returned to the veranda, Niko was leaning against one of the poles, his gaze on the far sea.

"Sorry about that," she said.

"You told her about the taverna. How did she take it?"

"She didn't faint."

Niko laughed. He then shifted his gaze to her. "Your friend found you a job?

"It's not guaranteed."

"I'm happy for you."

Olivia pressed her lips together. "Thanks," she said, but something inside her wilted at his words.

~~~~~~~~~~~~~~~~~~~~~~~~~~~~~~

On Monday morning, they lingered in bed. It was the least busy weekday at the taverna. But when Niko got ready to leave, Olivia insisted on joining him.

"You shouldn't spend your last days here working as a waitress."

She shushed him with a kiss and put on her blue dress. Having her makeup kit, contact lenses, and hair products meant Olivia felt more presentable. She left her hair down and arranged her curls. It was wild but not messy.

They passed by the regular alley-sitters, as Olivia started thinking of the elderly people who met daily for coffee and chat outside their houses' doors. She noticed how they glanced at her and Niko, although they kept a respectful distance from each other. Niko greeted them in Greek and exchanged a friendly sentence or two without stopping his stride.

He opened the taverna's door, and they walked in. It was the first time Olivia had been in it when it was so still and silent. The steady buzz of the coffee machine, the clanking sounds from the kitchen, the music in the background weren't there. When she helped Niko turn everything on and revive the place, she felt like she was helping to bring it to life. *It's silly*, she thought, but she couldn't help feeling that it made her an even deeper part of its pulse.

Taking her apron off the kitchen wall's hook and greeting the few regulars who arrived even on a Monday intensified that feeling. It had been two days since she had worked, and she was on a roll.

When Olivia took a break at table thirty-two, which she still referred to privately as *her* table, a text from Daria hit her inbox. It was six a.m. in Seattle, and Daria should be getting ready for a new work week.

"*I was serious the other day. I spent all evening searching for flights. What if I join you for the weekend in Corfu? We could fly back together on the following Monday.*"

"*OMG, really?*" Olivia texted back.

"*It's feasible. Should I book it?*"

"*Yes!*"

"*We could recreate Cancun in Corfu! Remember?! OMGGG! Will book and send you the details.*" Being spontaneous was Daria's expertise. Before Jeff and Olivia had sunk into early bourgeois, Daria had been able to drag Olivia to all kinds of fun.

"*Oh, I almost forgot! Feel like gloating?*" Another text from Daria arrived while Olivia was still searching for beach and sun emojis.

"*Gloating?*" Olivia typed instead.

"*Tyler spoke to Jeff. Guess who said the job in Boston wasn't what he thought it'd be?*"

Olivia's fingers hovered over the keyboard, but she didn't know what to type.

"*Come on! Karma is a bitch*," Daria typed.

"*I don't know.*"

"*Ok, ok, you're not one for gloating. I'll gloat for you.*"

"*LOL.*"

"*GTG, TTYL*," Daria signed off.

Olivia rubbed a hand over her mouth. Jeff's choice had impacted them both. She convinced herself that she had chosen, too, but the way he had gone about it hadn't left her a real choice. Now he seemed to regret that. His request to meet her suddenly took a different turn.

Only after she shut her phone and placed it facedown did Olivia realize with a sinking heart that the Monday that Daria had referred to was a week from today. Going then would give her a few days in Seattle before the ceremony, she was now forced to calculate. It seemed like a waste. She could let Daria go back alone and fly a day or two later. But having Daria with her when she would have to leave this place, leave Niko, could be her only saving grace. She would think about it later when Daria sent her the details. It may not happen after all.

Niko took advantage of the quiet hour and came to sit with her with two cups of steamy aromatic Greek coffee, which Olivia had taken a liking to by now.

"Niko," she sighed. "Daria wants to come here for the weekend. Is it okay if she came and stayed with me? I could take her to a hotel, too. It's just three nights, and then she has to fly back."

"Of course she can stay here. I'd like to meet her." Niko took a sip from his cup. "Won't you have to fly back, too, soon after, to make it to that ceremony?"

She took a deep breath and released it slowly. "Yeah, something like that."

"Time to go back to reality?" His eyes lingered on her before he looked away and stared at the street that reflected through the large window.

"It feels like *this* is reality," Olivia said, her eyes on his profile.

"It does," he agreed quietly.

~~~~~~~~~~~~~~~~~~~~~~~~~~~~~~~~~~

That night, she stayed at Niko's. Being the first to open the taverna the next day meant that no one would see her coming down from his apartment. But, somehow, she wasn't as pedantic about not being caught doing that. If Elena or Nina, or even one of the triplets saw her, she wouldn't care. Kostas, with his silent treatment of everyone but his wife and his few older friends, could make her more self-conscious, but he usually arrived in the afternoons.

She accidentally had the opportunity to test his reaction when, after a day of restraining herself from touching Niko in a way that would be too telling, at four, the in-between-customers hour, she went behind the bar with a stock of clean glasses. When she straightened up, she found herself facing Niko. He was so close, and the scent of his body made her almost drowsy. She smoothed a hand across his chest, her gaze devouring his lips. Then she leaned in just as Kostas entered through the back in his usual noisy manner. She flinched back, but he had already seen them; she was sure of it. He moved his eyes between them, and Niko didn't help either with the smirk that spread on his face. Olivia excused herself and disappeared into the kitchen.

That night, in his bed, she asked Niko if his family knew about them.

"Not officially, but they know."

She buried her face in his chest. "Yeah, Nina asked me about it on Sunday."

"Oh, if Nina asked, then everybody knows."

"She's not that much of a gossip. She only told me on Sunday that it was a tourists' car that …" Olivia faltered.

"That killed my parents?" he completed for her.

"Yes. It explains a lot, Niko."

"If you mean my dislike of a certain kind of tourists, then maybe. But I think that years of constantly representing my country and culture has more to do with it than anything else. And I really do love this place as it is and hope it will remain like that." After a moment's silence, he laughingly added, "So, it took Nina ten days of knowing you to tell you? That's progress."

"Come on; don't be so hard on her. She's great."

"I'm kidding. I love Nina. She's like another sister to me. We're closer in some ways than Cleo and I."

"I want to meet Cleo and Andreas." It came right out. No thought. No time to stop herself.

Niko looked at her. "You could. If you were here longer, you could go to Athens with me. I'll be there again later this month."

"I wish I could," she whispered. She didn't mean to whisper, but something pressed hard on her heart.

"Me, too. Maybe another time. Maybe when you come to Corfu as an expert in the hospitality industry." He poked her ribs, trying to lighten things up for her.

~~~~~~~~~~~~~~~~~~~~~~~~~~~~~

"I have to buy a solution for my contact lenses," Olivia said the next day. "I'll take the bus to Neo Limani."

"You can take my car."

"Thanks, but keep that green baby parked. I still don't trust myself with a stick shift on these narrow roads. Last time, I walked there."

On her way back to the bus stop after a short visit to the little pharmacy, Olivia observed a sign over one of the shops in the busy square of Neo Limani. "*Thalia's Art Gallery*," it read. She could recognize Thalia's style from the display in the window.

Hesitating for a second at the door, Olivia pushed it open and walked into the air-conditioned interior. The place was cleaner and more organized than the pharmacy that she had just left, and it looked effortlessly so.

There was no one there, so she walked around, admiring the paintings that hung on the walls and on a few easels that were calculatedly placed at certain points in the space.

"*Kalimera*. May I help you?"

Olivia turned.

"Oh, Olivia. Hello. Welcome." Thalia smiled widely and crossed the room toward her, flowing in a long flowery dress.

"*Kalimera*, Thalia. You have a beautiful place here."

"Thank you. Are you visiting Neo Limani?"

"I needed the pharmacy."

"How's Niko?"

"Okay, I think," Olivia replied, trying to deflect the significance of the question for the minuscule chance that Thalia didn't know about them.

"You know he's keeping an eye on the place for me when I'm gone? I give him my keys in case something happens. I had a break-in last year."

"I'm sorry. I didn't know." That explained the key exchange that she had witnessed and envied.

"They walked out with a fifty-euro bill and two of my least favorite paintings, so I didn't mind that much." Thalia's face lightened and became even more beautiful when she smiled. It was hard not to be jealous of her easy, cool confidence.

Olivia smiled back. "The painting that hangs over the fireplace in the house I borrow is one of my favorites, though you have very beautiful ones here, too."

"Thank you. Andreas and I painted that one."

"Niko told me you were Andreas's art therapist."

"I have something to show you," Thalia said, signaling Olivia to follow her. They went into a back room that served as an office. There were a few paintings there, including one that looked like a self-portrait of the artist. Thalia pointed at one of the paintings on the wall. "Recognize this?"

"Oh, wow. Teresi Taverna." Olivia's heart lurched as if she had recognized a familiar and beloved face in a crowd. "You know? It has always reminded me of Van Gogh's *Café Terrace At Night*, and you captured it well."

"Oh, thank you!" Thalia chuckled. "I'm no Van Gogh."

"No, I meant you captured the warmth of it, the welcoming. Like a haven."

"Is this how you feel about it?"

Olivia felt Thalia's gaze on her profile. She shifted her head to look at her. "Yes."

"Because of Niko?"

Olivia swallowed. She wanted to avert her gaze but couldn't. She wanted to lie but couldn't. "Yes."

"Interesting. I painted this seven years ago. He was still living abroad."

"Oh."

"You like him, don't you?"

Olivia hesitated. "Yes." Was Thalia using her therapeutic expertise on her? She felt compelled to volunteer the truth. It was hard not to.

"Can I be honest with you, Olivia?"

Olivia's heart plummeted to her stomach. "Sure."

"*I* like Niko. Everyone does. But looking at you, *you* don't just like him. Am I right?"

Olivia wasn't sure if she nodded or if any part of her moved.

Thalia went on, "He probably told you about us, and if he didn't, I'm sure Nina did. It was a long time ago and trifling. I don't think I've ever been in love, but I can tell when I see it on others. You know who I see it on?"

"Me?"

"Niko."

Olivia felt her own pulse thumping in her temples.

"Have you ever been in love?" Thalia asked.

"Yes."

"Are you sure? Because, if you were, you should be able to recognize it. Maybe it was too long ago?"

"Maybe."

Thalia tilted her head and observed Olivia as if she was deciphering an angle to paint her. "You don't say much, but you have a very honest face. You know why this painting is here?"

"Why?"

"Well, first because Niko didn't want it hanging at the taverna. Like his father, he, too, said it's silly to put a painting of the taverna in the taverna." Thalia chuckled. "But also because, when I was offering it for sale, no one described it as you just did. People saw it and asked if I had something that looked like those reproduced paintings of Parisian coffee shops or the taverna, but with the background of Mykonos." She ended with a scoff and a shake of her head. "Aleniki is a strange place to learn about the hospitality industry, Olivia. You should tell Niko why you're really staying."

Why *was* she staying? If it was only the conference fallout that kept her in Corfu, then the summit invitation and Daria's job prospect should have been the remedy. She should have booked a flight four days ago when she had first gotten the news, but she was still here and still hadn't.

Was Thalia right about the rest, too?

Everything in Thalia's words and interrogation was overwhelming. Persistent words echoed inside Olivia, ones she hadn't thought would echo there so soon or ever again. Words she couldn't admit if she wanted to go back to Seattle with her heart intact.

Instead, she forced herself to think about the fact that Niko had kept her secret even from Thalia, although the woman was shrewd enough to dismiss the explanation that he had invented for Olivia's presence. But knowing that didn't help Olivia's denial efforts; quite the contrary.

Chapter 15

She had always been good at suppressing feelings, truths, instincts, but this place forced them on her. Reality forced itself on her, too, especially in the last few days.

On Wednesday morning, Olivia shared with Niko the details of Daria's flight. They were in his bedroom, getting ready to go downstairs to open together. By now, Olivia assumed everyone knew they were spending their nights together either in his apartment or at the house. Her time with him was too limited to waste it on worrying. However, they still kept a respectful distance while in public.

"If I have to be in San Jose on Thursday and still make it to my apartment before, that means I need to leave here on Tuesday at the most. Daria flies back on Monday and wants me to go with her. But that extra day …"

Niko, dressed in one of his button-down shirts, its sleeves folded to his elbows in a way that made Olivia swoon, approached her. He took her in his arms and skimmed his gaze over her face. "Won't make a difference. I mean, it will, but it also won't."

"If I go back, I won't be able to come back here this summer. I'll have to find a job, and if Daria's pans out, I'll have to start working. *Have to*, I guess, is how it feels." She sighed.

"Don't you also *want* it? You didn't say much about that summit or the job, but …"

"I don't know anymore."

"I understand where you are, Olivia. I was there once. It wasn't just the suits and the diplomatic lingo that I had to shed, it was to learn to feel free from it inside. I didn't have to do, speak, or act like I was supposed to; I could do it all like I wanted to. And that's the key—I *wanted* to. But it took time to get there."

"I feel like I belong here. I … There's you." It was the closest to the truth. She was even more scared because of what now reflected in his eyes. There was no room for mistakes here. And there was too much on the line. What he said next verified it.

"I want you to stay, but you have to make sure you're not just replacing one sense of belonging with another. Otherwise, it's not real."

Olivia nodded, taking his words as a warning to not do something she might regret and cause damage to more than just herself.

Although the difference was just one day, when she navigated later to the airline website, Olivia prayed there wouldn't be seats on Daria's Monday flights. But there were, and she booked them, her eyes prickly with tears that she held back. Niko was right. One day didn't matter in the larger scheme of things.

~~~~~~~~~~~~~~~~~~~~~~~~~~~~~~~~

Once reality cracked and infiltrated her bubble, it didn't seem willing to stop.

That night, when Niko was in the kitchen, making them both a cup of herbal tea, and she was on the veranda, a text message from Jeff arrived.

The preview on her phone just indicated that it was a picture. Probably another internet quote. If she clicked on it, he would know she saw his message. Olivia tapped on it, hoping that, at the very least, it would be a useful quote, one that would provide applicable wisdom that she yearned for these days.

It opened. Austerely handsome with his blue eyes, smooth sandy hair, and the goatee he had been grooming in the last year, Jeff smiled at her from the living room of his Seattle apartment that used to be theirs. The caption read, *"It's not the same without you."*

Olivia gulped down the rakomelo that Niko had poured her before and shut the phone.

In the morning she found another text from Jeff. It was a meme of a cute cat with the caption, *"We need to talk."*

~~~~~~~~~~~~~~~~~~~~~~~~~~~~~~~

On one hand, Olivia couldn't wait for Daria to arrive. On the other, it meant the end of her stay. Having set a date, Olivia made the most of her time with Niko.

On Thursday, he let Kostas, Dimitrios, and two of the triplets run the busy taverna and took Olivia to a secret cove at the southwest tip of the island. All alone, hidden from sight in a natural rock formation that closed over them like a blue cave, they stripped each other from the swimsuits and made love in the water.

Held in his arms later, she trailed her fingertip over the tattoo on Niko's arm, from the green dot to the estimated location of the US west coast. If only the real distance was as small as it was in ink.

Later, they drove to Agios Gordios and spent the afternoon there, eating in a restaurant overlooking the sandy beach with its rocky bottom and million shades of blue.

She hadn't told him about Jeff's message, mainly because there wasn't much to tell. She hadn't bothered replying, and it hadn't moved her to feel anything except exasperation.

They made plans for Daria's arrival and stay but didn't speak about anything beyond Sunday until Niko brought up the week after when they strolled the beach of Pelekas at sunset.

"I was supposed to fly to Athens later next week, but I thought to move it forward. That way, I'll fly to Athens with you and Daria. What do you think?"

Her hand was held in his and, at this, Olivia halted her steps and pressed his palm. "Really?"

"I have to be there soon, anyway. That way, we get almost half a day together with all the security checks and the time until your international flight."

They stood in the middle of the walkway, surrounded by tourists and locals that, like them, enjoyed the breathtaking sunset over the sea. Someone's bag bumped into her as they sidestepped her and Niko, but Olivia didn't even notice. Her eyes were locked on Niko's, and she felt as if her heart was lodged in his chest rather than hers. The words were on her lips, and she wanted to utter them, but couldn't because … then what? It wouldn't be fair to either one of them if she said them, but she could now see what Nina and Thalia had told her—she could swear that the same words hovered over Niko's lips, and they were plain to read in his eyes. He pressed her palm back, and she knew that he could read them in her eyes, too.

"You'll come visit sometime, or I'll visit you," he said.

They both knew it didn't convey the depth of what they wanted or felt. They both knew it would have to be enough.

That night, in the bedroom of the house that overlooked the sea, Olivia clung to Niko and mouthed the words silently against his skin.

~~~~~~~~~~~~~~~~~~~~~~~~~~~~~

On Friday, a day after they had encircled the entire middle section of the island, they took the green car and drove directly into Corfu Town. After a stop at the bank for Niko, they drove to the airport to welcome Daria.

Olivia was excited as if she hadn't seen her friend in years. Her two and a half weeks in Greece seemed like two and a half years. It was as if she had built a life here—a house, a job, a community and, most importantly, Niko. It felt real. But it was temporary, borrowed. Only Niko was real. And, for him, Olivia knew her feelings weren't temporary. Their extent and magnitude frightened her.

Her palms sweated. This was Daria; there was no reason to be that nervous or excited. Only, when Olivia looked around her, at the tiny terminal with the signs written in Greek, the view of Corfu in the windows, and Niko beside her, she realized she was nervous and excited because Daria, who was a big part of her life in Seattle, came to mesh with the life she had created here. Two weeks' worth of life, and yet, a life. Adding Daria to it would make it complete.

"Oh, my God, your hair!" Were the first words that Daria uttered right after she had flung herself into Olivia's embrace. "You look wonderful! And so pretty like this!" She held Olivia's hand and forced her to twirl so she could see her from all angles.

"And you must be Niko." She turned to him. "I can't say I heard a lot about you, but the little this one was willing to share was enough. It's a pleasure to meet you." She gave Niko a sturdy handshake.

Niko took hold of Daria's luggage and let the two women walk ahead of him, chattering excitedly.

"What do you know? No delays, *and* I got my luggage," Daria said, laughing. "How come these things only happen to you?" She poked Olivia's side. "But look what that turned into," she whispered close to Olivia's ear. "Oh, my God, this man! And that accent! I'd lose my luggage and wear any ugly shirt, if I could meet someone like that."

Olivia laughed. "I have so much to tell you."

After a lively drive back to Aleniki, with Olivia joining Niko in indicating points of interest along the way, Niko dropped them off at the main square. They made their way to the house together while he went to the taverna to give them some alone time.

Daria praised every pebble, bougainvillea, and house on the way and reached a high-pitched voice at the sight of the house that Olivia was staying in. "I want to move here! Oh, my God, you're so lucky!"

"I didn't feel lucky when you know what happened," Olivia reminded her.

"Oh, yes, well, except for that part and the getting laid off part. But I hope getting properly *laid* by that hunk made up for at least some of it."

Olivia sighed. "That's the part I've been dying to talk to you about. Go pee—you said you have to—and we'll talk later."

On the veranda, after ten minutes of admiring the view, circling the house, and applauding every nook and cranny, Daria finally sat down with a glass of rakomelo that Olivia had poured her from a bottle that Niko had brought over a few days before.

"Oh, that's yummy. What do you call it again? Rocket Melon?"

"Rakomelo." Olivia laughed. She then told her everything, ending with Jeff's text and Niko's change of flights to Monday so they would have a bit more time together.

"You love him." It was a statement.

Olivia's jaw muscle twitched. Finally, the words had been uttered, even if it wasn't her that had said them.

"I'm not asking. I see it. I haven't seen you like this in so many years. Maybe not ever. Not like this. You're glowing. And the way you look at him, and all those little couple-y touches of you two. I saw it right away. Have you told him?"

"No. What would be the point?"

"Um, I don't know." Daria rolled her eyes upward as if she was really looking for the answer. "Maybe if you feel that way toward someone, you'd better tell them?"

"I'm leaving in three days, Daria."

"I think he feels the same," Daria went on, ignoring her. "I don't know him, but from everything you told me, this doesn't sound like a man who's having a fling with a nice tourist. He lets you stay in his family's house; he brings you into his family, not just his taverna; he takes you into his bed and not in a wham-bam-thank-you-ma'am sort of way, he wants you to stay the night; he just drove all the way to pick up your friend from the airport; and he's taking time off to spend it with you and that friend." She pointed at herself mockingly. "And you said he doesn't want you to leave. I don't know … It sounds serious to me."

Olivia sighed. "That's the problem. That's why I don't say it." She missed talking to Daria, who could usually bring back sense and perspective into everything, though now the picture she had painted didn't make Olivia's life any easier.

"And Jeff … Oh, come on. Do I really have to say it?" Daria went on.

"No." Olivia scratched her forehead. "I didn't even reply. Water under the bridge. He regrets the job; he doesn't regret me. Besides, too little, too late. It's just that—"

"It's just that what?" Daria cut her off. "If you wanted him, and the only thing that stood in your way was your job in Seattle, then what stopped you from getting on the first plane to Boston to be with him once Doreen fired you?"

"Daria, you're preaching to the choir. I know all that, though it took me time to realize it. I don't want him. I don't feel anything for him. It's gone. I was just going to use it as an example. That, with Jeff's message and the award ceremony and the job with Uno, it's like I can have my old life back almost the same as it was, but I'm not sure I want it anymore."

"I can't blame you. Being here, I can see why you're confused."

"The thing is that I'm not confused. I know how I feel. But this isn't just the other side of the country. This is the other side of the world. What am I going to do, Daria?"

"Have fun with me this weekend. The rest will figure itself out."

"Now, if Jeff had sent *this* with a cat picture, I'd have his kids," Olivia said, and they both rolled with laughter.

~~~~~~~~~~~~~~~~~~~~~~~~~~~~~~~~~~~

Later that evening, they went to the taverna. Olivia's heart skipped a beat, as always, at the sight of Niko behind the bar. His effect on her hadn't changed despite the expectation of finding him there.

He treated her and Daria to drinks. "I saved you your table," he said to Olivia, his warm smile surging through her, affirming that he, too, thought of it as hers.

For the first time in weeks, Olivia sat as a guest in the taverna again. However, she didn't allow anyone to wait on them but served the food and drinks for her and Daria herself. While she was in the kitchen, she took out plates that were waiting there and served them to a table outside. Then she carried two drinks from the bar to a nearby table while bringing another round for her and Daria.

"You really *do* work here as a waitress," Daria commented when Olivia rejoined her.

"Volunteer, help. I don't know if I could do it as a permanent thing, but every now and then, like Nina or the triplets, I wouldn't mind." Though Daria hadn't met everyone yet, Olivia had told her all about them. "How about that food?"

"It's great. What am I eating?"

Olivia named the dishes for her and told her about her favorites.

She caught Daria staring at her instead of the plate at some point. "What?"

"Nothing. I just enjoy seeing you like this," Daria replied with a little smile.

Olivia didn't know if it was Niko's initiation or not but, at some point, after most people finished eating and Olivia and Daria put a fifty euros bill under a plate for Althea to find later, more people arrived for drinks, including Elena, Kostas, and even Nina and her husband. Someone took out a bouzouki and another extricated a baglama, and spontaneous music and dancing ensued.

Olivia had the pleasure of introducing Daria to Elena, Nina, and even Kostas, as well as two of the triplets who were working. She also had the painful mission of telling them that she was going away on Monday and watching the genuine regret on their faces.

"I hoped for something else," Nina told her when no one noticed them. "I think Niko is very sad about it. He doesn't say, but I'm sure."

Like she had learned already, things that were only whispered internally became real when uttered out loud. Nina's simple words removed the veil of repression that Olivia had tried hard to keep on. A weight sat on her chest during the happy dances that she and Daria were dragged to. A mist of sadness separated her from the gleeful room. She watched through barely-noticing eyes Daria being Daria and having fun and dancing like she had been born in Greece. Only when she met Niko's glance did she feel like she wasn't alone in it, but that only made it worse.

That night, after she saw Daria into the house, she asked for her permission to leave her alone there. "I have to go to Niko. I can't stand not being with him."

"I'm so beat that I'm falling asleep as you speak. Go," Daria slurred.

Olivia made her way back to the main street, circled the taverna to the back of the building, went upstairs, and knocked on his door. The moment he opened the door, shirtless, she threw herself into Niko's arms. They didn't speak that night, at least not with words.

Chapter 16

When Olivia went back to the house the next morning, Daria was still asleep. An hour later, they were both showered and ready for a tour of their side of the island. Niko took the morning off, and they joined him at the village square. They took Daria to the secret cove.

When they were in the water, Olivia told Daria about her first visit to a beach in Corfu, where she had wished she had been with her so she would have the courage to go into the water without formal swimwear.

"Ah, but what about the famous bikini bottom instead of clean underwear?" Daria chuckled.

"It was one of the first things I knew about her," Niko said, grabbing Olivia by her waist, hoisting her over to him, then pressing a kiss on her lips.

"Hey, hey, you'll get a room later." Daria spritzed water at them.

"I like your friend," Niko whispered to Olivia later. "It's good that you're flying back with her." He didn't have to say more for them both to know what he meant.

"So, Niko, do you have any brothers you could introduce me to? Cousins can fit, as well," Daria joked when they sat at a beach restaurant later.

Olivia hadn't chanced telling her about Andreas's condition yet and now awkwardly looked at Niko, but he didn't seem fazed.

"I have one brother, but he's unwell. I do have a million first and second cousins, and I even think some of them are unmarried," he replied with a smile.

Daria threw a glance at Olivia, as if asking *why didn't you warn me?* but she went on with, "Can you think of anyone who'll be willing to make an honest woman out of me and grant me citizenship while he's at it?"

Niko laughed. "Let me sleep on it," he said, wrapping an arm around Olivia.

She didn't know if Daria did it on purpose or not, but that hit too close to home, as Daria's words often did.

~~~~~~~~~~~~~~~~~~~~~~~~~~~~

They all agreed that Niko would drop them off at Neo Limani village so Daria could buy presents.

"I hope you, ladies, will excuse me, but shopping is beyond my pay grade," he jested. "Call me, and I'll pick you up when you're done," he added to Olivia.

Taking Daria to all the tourists' souvenir shops, buying shot glasses, mugs, snow globes, and other Corfu-branded knickknacks, Olivia didn't feel like a tourist but as a local escorting one. The only things she bought were a scarf for her mother and a hand-painted paperweight for her father.

When they strolled the main square, her eyes were drawn to Thalia's gallery.

"Remember I told you about Thalia?" she asked Daria. "That's her art gallery over there. Let's go in. There's a painting there I want to look at again."

"Oh, I want to see her. I didn't know it was this village."

Thalia was busy with a customer when they walked in.

"Hi, Olivia," she called with a smile.

"Can I show her—"

"Of course." Thalia had immediately understood.

Olivia took Daria to see the painting of the taverna and half-whispered the conversation she'd had with Thalia about it.

"Nice to meet you. I'm Thalia." Thalia extended her hand toward Daria with her usual grace the moment the customer left.

Daria introduced herself as Olivia's friend and added a compliment about the gallery. "I recognize your style from the paintings in the house at Aleniki."

"How much would you charge for this one, Thalia?" Olivia went straight to the point though she hadn't planned it when she had come in.

"You want it?"

"I'm leaving on Monday, and this could be …"

"A memento for the real thing," Thalia muttered. "It's fifty euros," she said louder.

The paintings that were offered for sale in the front room had price tags on them and only a few smaller ones carried that price; certainly not those that were twenty by twenty-eight inches.

"Come on, Thalia. What is it with this island?" Olivia said.

"It's not the island; it's Aleniki. I don't live there, but I love it. We value other things. Says the woman who has a gallery in the next village to make money," Thalia said with a charming self-deprecating laugh. "It's fifty."

Olivia wanted to hug her, though the *we* in Thalia's words was like a punch to the gut. To be included in the Aleniki *"we"* was a privilege she envied.

"I'll pay a hundred-fifty. No argument," she said.

Thalia bubble-wrapped it for her. "Niko will be happy you have it," she said, looking at Olivia. "Some things are worth the wait."

"Thank you." She wanted to say more but was tongue-tied once again. "For everything," she added, hoping Thalia would comprehend.

"She's pretty. I can see why you were worried," Daria said when they walked toward the bus station. Olivia didn't want to bother Niko to pick them up. "I hope I look like her fifteen years from now. And she's very kind. They're all great. That conference screw-up is possibly the best thing that ever happened to you, you know that? You have me to thank for that."

Olivia's laughter choked in her throat.

~~~~~~~~~~~~~~~~~~~~~~~~~~~~~~~~~

That evening, Olivia had a mini-preview of what it would be like to say goodbye to Niko when she had to bid all the others farewell. A few tears escaped their prison and streamed down her face as she hugged Elena, shook hands with Kostas, and kissed Nina goodbye. She put the envelope that Elena had shoved into her hand into the top drawer of the kitchen employees' cabinet so that they would find it on Monday.

Trailing her fingertip over her name in Greek at the edge of the laminated picture, she then moved it to caress Niko's photographed smiling face.

~~~~~~~~~~~~~~~~~~~~~~~~~~~~~~

"Check this out. As if," Olivia scoffed, handing Daria her phone as they stood outside the taverna and breathed in the night air, waiting for Niko to lock up.

"*Tell Daria I said hi. I'd be with you there if I didn't have to be back in Boston*," Daria read Jeff's new text out loud.

"Damn Tyler. He can't keep anything to himself," Daria said. "If I understand correctly, Jeff's days in Boston are numbered. He'll be back in Seattle, and then he'll try to make you take him back. You should tell him what he can do with his hints."

"Better yet, I'll send him a meme," Olivia replied.

"That's my girl!" Daria wrapped her arm around Olivia's shoulders and squeezed her.

"That's *my* girl," they heard a male voice, and before they managed to turn more than their heads, Niko wrapped his arms around Olivia's waist from behind and planted a kiss on her neck.

She gave the house keys to Daria, and they bid each other goodnight, having agreed in advance that

Daria would stay alone at the house so that Olivia and Niko could spend their last few nights together.

~~~~~~~~~~~~~~~~~~~~~~~~~~~~~~~~~~~~

"How did you do it, Niko?" she asked much later, leaning her head on his shoulder in the darkened bedroom of his apartment. "How did you uproot yourself, and then again?"

"It's not easy, and it's not always clear cut, but I think that it's a balance that shifts, and then you just know. It can take time. For me, the definition of happiness and purpose changed, and the importance of people, money, prestige, ambition, success. And I just knew. It wasn't immediate, but maybe that's why it's lasting."

Olivia shifted her head and planted a kiss on his chest, feeling the thump of his heart beneath the warm skin. She pressed her cheek to it, wishing that the seismic shifts of her life had been less painful.

~~~~~~~~~~~~~~~~~~~~~~~~~~~~~~~~~~~~

Olivia could almost physically feel the draining of the sand in the hourglass. If before she hadn't counted the days because she didn't want to know, now she counted the hours and minutes.

Niko fixed the three of them breakfast in the closed taverna on Sunday morning—that deducted ninety minutes from her time with him. They drove to Sidari and spent the morning in Kanali Tu Erota and Paleokastritsa—that equaled seven hours. They went back to Aleniki so she could pack while Niko sat on the veranda with Daria, who hadn't even unpacked—that was thirty minutes off her last day with him.

She almost regretted having Daria there, but Daria being Daria had booked a local taxi without telling them and announced she was going to Neo Limani to spend the evening.

"There's one thing I still haven't done on this island," she said with a wink. "I mean mixing ouzo with water, obviously."

That night was a night of lasts—making use of the bedroom in the house one last time, curling up against Niko on the veranda one last time, spending the night together one last time.

When they prepared to go back to his apartment after Daria's return, Olivia rolled her trolley out of the bedroom, carrying the wrapped painting under her arm.

"You bought it?" Niko asked when he noticed it. "I completely forgot about this painting."

"I had to. Just so I have it until I see the original again."

"You will."

"Promise?" she asked, though she was the one leaving. It was as if she was grasping for strength, because she didn't find it within her.

"I do. Do you?" Niko said.

"I do."

Daria, who tried to absent herself while they spoke, entered through the large glass door that connected the living room and the veranda just in time to hear the last part of their conversation. "By the power vested in me, I now pronounce you. You may kiss."

A faint laugh escaped Olivia's and Niko's lips.

Daria disappeared into the bedroom that she had been occupying and left them to stare at one another.

That night, they clung to each other as if Daria hadn't mischievously cut the original sentence.

~~~~~~~~~~~~~~~~~~~~~~~~~~~~~

They had an hour before having to leave for Corfu airport, and Niko stored their trolleys in the back seat and trunk of the car while they waited for Daria.

Although he usually opened late on Monday, Niko and Olivia entered the taverna from the back.

"Should we open?" she asked.

"No. Elena will open later. I just want to show you something."

"What is it?"

He took her hand and walked her to the middle of the space, facing the bar. "Look over there," he said.

Olivia skimmed her eyes over the bar. Everything looked the same, except that it was silent. Then she raised her eyes. "Oh, wow," she called. The menu was written in English next to Greek. "Who did this?" She looked at Niko, who stood beside her, smiling. By now, she had known what his handwriting looked like in both English and Greek.

"Since I wasn't around, I asked Althea to do it yesterday. We could be a little more welcoming here, though I don't promise to do this every day."

"Of course not. That would be too much," she teased, then kissed him.

"I have one more thing for you."

"What?"

"*Siga, siga*," he said, taking her hand and walking her to the kitchen. It was a common expression that she had heard before, one that someone like her could benefit from. It meant "*slowly, slowly*" and applied to how life should be lived.

Next to the laminated picture on the kitchen wall, the one she had written her name on in Greek, was a new laminated picture that had been taken at the wedding on her first night helping out. The photographer had captured her and Niko during the dance. Their names were printed on it in Greek.

"I saw you staring at that picture once," Niko said, pointing at the staff picture, "so I tried to figure out what you saw in it and noticed you wrote your name. I called the groom, asked him to send me a link to their pictures, and found this."

Olivia covered her mouth, trying to hold back the overflowing emotions that threatened to burst out of her. Then she wrapped her arms around Niko, who enveloped her entirely.

"Thank you." She exhaled against his chest.

"No crying in Elena's kitchen," he whispered into her hair.

Olivia laughed despite herself. She raised her face to him, and their kiss mixed with the salt of her tears.

She didn't reveal that she, too, had left him something in the house's bedroom closet. The "*I heart Greece*" T-shirt with a handwritten note that contained two words in the Greek alphabet—his name and the word "*S'agapo*," which was the translation of the three English words she yearned to tell him.

~~~~~~~~~~~~~~~~~~~~~~~~~~~~~~~~~~

Like the day three weeks before, when she had been prepared to leave and Niko had offered to drive her to the airport, Olivia was now thankful to have a few more hours with him.

Almost no words were exchanged as they went through security and the flight together. She rested her head on Niko's shoulder and watched the green island becoming smaller and smaller until it disappeared from view. She knew she would be leaving a part of her there, but it hurt much more than she had expected.

Daria was unusually silent, as well.

~~~~~~~~~~~~~~~~~~~~~~~~~~~~~~~~~~

After picking up their luggage in Athens, they had an hour before she and Daria would have to go through the international flight process.

"I have to look at these shops, and I'm hungry. Are you hungry?" Daria excused herself, obviously trying to leave them alone.

"It was a pleasure meeting you, Daria," Niko said. "I hope to see you again, too. Take good care of this one," he added, tilting his head with a smile toward Olivia.

"I will," Daria replied. Instead of a formal handshake, she hugged Niko, and he kissed her on both cheeks like an old friend.

~~~~~~~~~~~~~~~~~~~~~~~~~~~~~~

"Niko."

"Olivia."

They looked at each other, and it was so momentous and dramatic that they both scoffed then started laughing, because there was nothing left to do. They laughed so hard that they grabbed each other's arms, bending over, until tears rolled down Olivia's cheeks.

"No, Niko, really," she gasped, trying to stop the hysteric laughter, which was too close to turning into a sob. "Remember you said you like people who make mistakes?"

"Yes," Niko said, gaining control of his laughter.

"What if I'm making a mistake here, will you still like me?"

They were both serious now, as if they hadn't just gone through a feat of laughter.

"I don't just like you, Olivia."

"I don't just like you, too, Niko."

"I know."

"You do, huh?"

"Buying that painting gave you in," he said. She could see the jesting glint in his eyes even before his smile gave him away.

"I *will* be back, as soon as I can, and I hope you'll still want me here."

"Always."

"Don't say always before you know when it'll be."

"I still say always."

Olivia leaned against the wall behind her, and Niko caressed her face and hair, pressing his other palm on the wall beside her head. His gaze caressed her, too.

For her, everything else was gone—the endless flight and no smoking announcements in Greek and English, the passengers that hurried past them, the sound of a million tiny suitcase wheels rolling. All she could see was his face. She could drown in his eyes.

Niko bent and kissed her long and deep. Olivia fisted his shirt at the back, pressing him closer against her.

He leaned his forehead against hers. "You have everything you need?" His voice was husky.

She nodded.

"Let me know when you land."

She nodded again.

"You'll tweet your presentation?" he asked, smiling softly.

"I hope no one else does," she replied, trying to smile back.

"You'll do great. Just make sure your messenger is closed and that Daria is nowhere near an internet connection."

He could make her laugh even now.

"Niko." She bent forward and leaned her forehead against his chest.

Niko rubbed his palm over her nape then weaved his fingers into her hair. "I'll be here," he said, then kissed the crown of her head.

Why did she have to fall in love with a man who lived on the other side of the earth?

"Hey, guys. Olivia," they heard Daria gently interrupting some time after. "Our flight was announced. We have to check in very soon."

Olivia's face was still buried in Niko's chest. He said something to Daria, but she couldn't make out the words. She was consumed in fighting herself. Every fiber in her begged her to cancel everything, throw it all to hell, and just stay with him here. But the lingering damage caused by years of rigidly toeing the line, meeting expectations, prioritizing practicalities over emotions, instincts, wants—kept her mute.

"*Antio, agapi mou,*" Niko whispered in her ear, and the fist around her heart hurt so much that she couldn't bring herself to speak.

She understood enough Greek to know that *antio* meant *goodbye*, *mou* meant *my*, and *agapi* was some derivative of the word *agape—love*.

Teary eyes and silence were all she was capable of, inwardly hating herself for not telling him that she loved him, too.

Chapter 17

Olivia had no idea how she had gotten on the plane; all she remembered was giving Niko one last tear-stained kiss and an endless roaming in large, fluorescent-lit halls and corridors, mechanically following Daria's footsteps.

Only after takeoff was Olivia able to speak again. No one sat next to them, and Daria had wrapped her arm around her shoulders and let Olivia rest her head against hers.

"I think he wanted to spare *you*, Olivia, probably for the same reason you didn't tell *him*. He didn't want you to do something you weren't a hundred percent sure of, so he said it only when there was nothing to lose. He put you before himself."

"Damn, Daria." It came out as a whisper as Olivia wiped the tears that reached her chin.

"I only say it as I see it. Livvy, don't beat yourself up. I'm all talk, but I would have done the same thing—go back home. Most people would."

"I should have told him."

"It's not too late. But I think he knows. Everyone who saw you there knew." Daria let out a sad, little chuckle and rubbed Olivia's arm. "Oh, sweetie, I'm sorry. I feel like it's all my fault again. You ended up there because of me and met a wonderful man who happens to live on the other side of the world."

"It's not fair."

"It's not. But you know what? Give it a few more days, weeks if you can, and see how you feel. Maybe the distance will …"

Olivia shook her head under Daria's chin.

"Okay. If you still feel like that in a few days, you and I will have a little chat. Okay?"

~~~~~~~~~~~~~~~~~~~~~~~~~~~~~~~

Seattle's evening sky welcomed them with rain when they finally landed after the long flight that included a layover in New York.

For most of the haul, Olivia hadn't spoken much. She had either stared out the window or slept, purposefully numbing her brain and trying to control her heart after the initial outburst.

"We're home," Daria said, turning her phone on as soon as they stepped onto the jet bridge.

Olivia didn't reply.

"*We landed*," she typed on her phone. It was the middle of the night in Greece, for the only person whose voice she wanted to hear.

~~~~~~~~~~~~~~~~~~~~~~~~~~~~~~~

Everything looked familiar and strange at the same time. It was as if she was a visitor with a critical eye looking at the city center, the skyscrapers, the wet sidewalks, her building, the tired woman with the frizzy hair that reflected through the elevator's mirror.

Olivia fished out the keys from her backpack and unlocked her apartment door. A stale smell hit her nostrils. The place had been closed for twenty-three days. Good thing she didn't have any plants there.

Leaving her suitcase and the painting in the middle of the living room, she opened several windows. Her next stop was the refrigerator where she threw out what little she found in it and tied the bin bag, her mind wandering to the fridge in the house in Aleniki and Elena's takeout boxes.

~~~~~~~~~~~~~~~~~~~~~~~~~~~~~~

Practical tasks usually served her best. Olivia took a shower, changed the sheets on her bed, unpacked, prepared a laundry basket to take to the washing machines at the building's basement the next day, and went to bed. After some tossing and turning, she finally succumbed to sleep.

The anemic sunrays that infiltrated her bedroom woke her up at seven a.m. It took her a moment to realize she wasn't in the house or Niko's apartment in Aleniki.

A text from Niko awaited on her phone, the first thing she grabbed.

"*Good morning, glykia mou. I hope everything's ok and that you have coffee.*"

Olivia let out a sad scoff. He had called her "my sweet" and knew her state in the mornings.

Making coffee and taking it without milk, still numb, she called her mother to let her know she had arrived.

"Mom, I'm jet-lagged. I'll talk to you later," she hurried to sign off.

She wasn't jet-lagged. It was just that there was a pain in her heart the size of Corfu and the shape of Niko.

With a nine-hour difference, it was early evening in Greece. She called Niko, but not via video, as she was tempted to do, knowing that seeing him would only hurt more.

He picked up after two rings. "Hey, beautiful," he said, and her heart clenched.

"*Kalispera*, Niko."

"You sound tired. Jet-lagged?"

"No. Missing you."

"I miss you, too. I told Cleo about you yesterday." He breathed. "I'm almost at Andreas's now. I'll tell him you said hi." She could hear his smile over the phone. He was still trying to lighten things up for her.

"Please do."

He asked about the flights and how she was adjusting to being back home. Talking to him, hearing his voice, made the thousands of miles that stretched between them achingly palpable. It was more painful than it had been when she had moved out of the apartment that she and Jeff had shared for seven out of their ten years together.

"Niko, you know I feel the same way, right?" She knew he would understand what she was referring to.

"Pretty much." After a pause, he added, "I just got to Andreas's. I'll talk to you tomorrow, okay?"

"Sure. Bye, Niko."

Laundry, a little grocery shopping that would last for a few days before she would have to leave for

San Jose, ensuring her flight there was confirmed, emailing through her private laptop with Lynn from the summit's organizing committee, handling online paperwork related to her layoff, and other mundane tasks kept Olivia comfortably numb for most of the day. Exchanging a few lines with Daria and again ensuring her mother that she was working on her presentation and securing the job with Uno were the only interruptions.

And all that time, she knew exactly what hour it was in Greece, and her mind kept calculating what was happening at the taverna and wondering how Niko was doing in Athens.

She survived her first day away from him, the first out of who-knew-how-many.

~~~~~~~~~~~~~~~~~~~~~~~~~~~~~~~~~~

All of Wednesday morning, Olivia worked to recreate her presentation from memory. Going through everything again—all the principles and practices that she had implemented at DoITmore and the main messages that she had been planning to convey at the conference in Greece—reminded her that she still believed in the values and ideals that had led her to choose Human Resources as a career path.

She had chosen it despite her mother's insistent advice that she should go for engineering or finance. It wasn't thanks to her own company that had betrayed her and those principles, but thanks to Niko and his family's taverna that she could still believe that these values were valid, true, and applicable in every type of business, because they all dealt with *human* resources.

She had a meeting with Kaylin, Daria's friend from Uno, and a representative from their HR department to discuss the job they had to offer. It sounded right up her alley and was an advancement in comparison to what she had done at Teamtastic, as was the salary they offered. They both expressed disgust at what had happened to her at the conference and ended the meeting with a promise for a formal job offer letter.

Three weeks ago, she would have considered her cup "runneth over" at all this, but now none of it made the slightest impact on her heart. All the pieces of her old life were coming together and were made available to her again, but she no longer wanted them.

Numbly, she packed for San Jose. Not the grey pencil skirt suit, though; she couldn't even look at that one. Instead, she packed a regular black pant suit and, at the last moment, threw in the "*I heart Greece*" T-shirt that Daria had bought her as a private joke and memento when she had rambled the airport shops alone while Olivia had been busy breaking her own and Niko's hearts. Then she reorganized her backpack to ensure everything she needed for the short flight and one night stay at the San Jose hotel was there.

At various nooks of the bag, she found receipts from the shops in Paleokastritsa and Neo Limani, bus tickets, and brochures that had been shoved into her hand while she had strolled Corfu Town. Each one of them carried a memory. Each added to her longing and accentuated her ache.

Sliding her laptop into the special case inside the bag that had contained her Teamtastic laptop before she had given it over to Lee, Olivia noticed a crackling sound. Reaching in, she found a piece of paper that had been pushed down by her laptop. She fished it out and straightened it. It was a simple notebook page in Niko's handwriting. He must have slipped it in there when she hadn't noticed.

> *Olivia,*
>
> *If I didn't think it would confuse or pressure you even more, I'd tell you the things this note says while you were still here.*
>
> *S'agapo, Olivia. That means I love you.*
>
> *If I didn't think it would confuse you further, I'd follow you.*
>
> *If you find that you're happy where you are and still want it, I'll come to you.*
>
> *We can find a way.*
> *Niko.*

If she wasn't already seated, Olivia would have folded into the sofa. As it was, her hands holding the note fell limp to her sides. She stared at the blank wall across the room from her before she brought the note in front of her eyes and read it again. Her hand rose by itself to cover her mouth.

She was afraid of making mistakes, yet here she was, making the biggest mistake of her life. Every ounce of being in her wanted Niko and, by some luck or destiny, he wanted her just the same. All of this was hers, and she had rejected it, and for what?

A glitch, a fiasco her mother had called the kismet that made Olivia feel happy, alive, free, and the most in love she had ever been. But that glitch made her recalculate her route.

At the age of thirty-eight, it wasn't just a job that she had lost but an ideology. She had believed and become and belonged to the trajectory she had been on. It had become an aim by itself, served by her career and relationship, and eventually by her happiness, which she had lost sight of. Sticking with it had meant something, like her parents and she, herself, had always expected of her. But not anymore. Not after what she had discovered in that place and with this man. It wasn't like anything she had ever experienced or felt. Not even close.

What if this *could* be her reality? Niko and Corfu had already *felt* real. They *were* real. She could make them *her* reality. She wanted to. And when it came to Niko, she n*eeded* to. If there was anything she wanted and needed to believe, become, and belong to, it was him.

It was the middle of the night in Greece or she would have called him to tell him that she loved him, too. He couldn't have found the note that she had left in the closet in Aleniki since he was still in Athens. She should have told him before when he held her in his arms, in his bed, at the airport—anywhere.

When she had full control of her senses again, Olivia opened a new, private Twitter account and sent an invite to Daria and Niko with a simple message. "*I'll live stream my presentation here.*"

Daria's reply came right away. "*I promise to stay away from messenger this time. Good luck, Livvy. You got this.*"

Niko's came in when she was on the flight to San Jose, and she only saw it later. "*Can't wait to see your face again. I know you'll rock this.*"

Chapter 18

Just before eight p.m., Olivia made sure that both Niko and Daria were connected to her account and that Lynn from HR4Excellence was seated in the front row, holding Olivia's phone and live-streaming. Only then did Olivia go on the stage in front of the five hundred attendees at the elegant hall in San Jose Olive Tree Hotel.

Her laptop was connected to the large screen, and her presentation header was shown.

Give Tech A Break
Olivia Duncan

"Good evening, everyone. Thank you, Lynn and the organizing committee for having me here. Lynn wanted to introduce me, but since you're all from the various venues of HR, you probably know me already from the videos that were posted to Twitter almost a month ago from a hall very much like this one. You probably know more about me than I'd normally be willing to share on a stage."

The audience chuckled and clapped for her.

"Yes, that was fun," she added with a smile, running a hand through her curls. "What followed on Twitter, and in my own company, was so much fun that it made me doubt, distrust, and eventually reevaluate the ideals that had led me into Human Resources in the first place. Maybe I owe those people thanks." Olivia chuckled nervously. "Not really. My thanks goes to one person who, in less than a week, restored my faith in what I've been helping my customers implement for a decade. Most of you know the Three B's. Well, this man made me believe, become, and belong to a workplace again, to a community, though I was a mere stranger."

Olivia paused. "I had about twenty slides for you in my original presentation, but I bet you'd appreciate getting to the refreshments bar earlier." She clicked her laptop and opened a slide that had one sentence written on it. "These ten words summarize my entire one-hour speech. You can take it or leave it. It shouldn't be news to you. People hire consultants to tell them what they already know." Olivia pointed at the screen. "*Treat your employees as you'd like to be treated yourself*," she read. "It applies to all situations, especially in a crisis." Olivia directed her eyes at the crowd.

The audience hesitated, but a few people yelled, "Yeah!" and began clapping. The entire hall followed through.

"Since I provided such entertainment and sensation recently," Olivia continued, "let me throw in some more. I have one more slide." Olivia took off her jacket and revealed the white T-shirt she was wearing beneath—the "*I heart Greece*" shirt that Daria had bought her.

"I put so much focus on professional achievements, maybe because I didn't have many other significant achievements to speak for. I clung to them and was scared shitless to lose them. But, once I did lose them, or thought I did, I learned their real value, and it wasn't as big as I thought it was. They're replaceable. I can find them somewhere else, maybe in the hospitality industry." She chuckled, trying to fight the tears that were clogging her throat and the clutching nervousness at doing this in front of so many people. "But there are some things that aren't replaceable; some things it's worth crossing the world to have and to hold."

She then clicked on her last slide. It was written in the Greek alphabet and contained the two words she had left in the note in the closet at the house, the one Niko hadn't had a chance to see.

"Niko," she said, "*efkharisto poly*, for everything. I have a lot to tell you, but mainly that there's nothing I want more, and nothing else I *need*, other than you. *S'agapo*, Niko. I love you." She directed her eyes at her phone that Lynn was holding, praying that Niko was watching this. "*You're* not replaceable, Niko. There's only one *you.* The balance has shifted, and I want to be where you are."

She didn't even notice that the women who made up the majority of the audience were up on their feet, clapping and cheering. She didn't care that a few people were holding phones and filming her.

"Thank you and sorry, Lynn, for hijacking the stage. Love is the real achievement that I wanted to talk about tonight. Believe, become, belong to it. Goodnight, everyone. And Niko, please don't go anywhere." With that, Olivia disconnected her laptop, grabbed it, and rushed off the stage.

Lynn met her at the side while the large room buzzed with people's excited voices. "Congratulations, Olivia. I think we are all walking out of here tonight with a useful and important message. And congratulations on finding love. I hope Niko appreciates how lucky he is."

"I'm the lucky one. Thank you, Lynn." She hugged the woman and kissed her on both cheeks before rushing outside while booking an Uber.

~~~~~~~~~~~~~~~~~~~~~~~~~~~~~~~~~~

Olivia's phone rang right when she was about to call Niko. She wanted to know if he watched, wanted to know if he had changed his mind. But it was Daria who was calling.

"Oh, my God, Livvy, what are you doing to my heart? That was amazing! I'm so proud of you. Niko must be ecstatic."

"God, I hope so. I haven't spoken to him yet. I hope he didn't change his mind."

"No way! He loves you."

"I shouldn't have left Greece in the first place."

"No, that's not true, and Niko would agree with me on this one. You *had* to go back to figure everything out. Didn't you tell me that's how he did it—went back to work then knew he should be somewhere else?"

"Yes. You're right. I have to talk to him, though."

"I bet, if you don't go there, he'll come here."

"I want to be there with him. I'm happier there, Daria."

"Can't blame you. But you have to tell your parents."

"I know. I will. They'll just have to accept that, if Niko is willing to have me, I'm moving to Greece."

"Damn, I have to find me a Niko," Daria said, laughing. "Now, go call him."

As soon as they hung up, the phone rang again. This time, it was Niko.

"How soon can you be here?" he asked the moment she picked up.

"Niko! I'm so glad you said that. I was standing there in front of you and everyone and hoping to God you didn't change your mind. I mean, you had time to think."

"If anything, it's the opposite. I had time to miss you even more."

"I'll go pack, arrange a few things, and get on the first reasonable flight. I might still catch you in Athens."

"I'll wait here. Elena and Kostas have everything under control, as usual."

"Okay. I can't wait to see you. I love you, Niko. I'm sorry I didn't say it earlier. I *did*, but not out loud. You're talking to a woman who didn't move across the same country, but to be with you, I don't care how far I have to go. Lucky me, you're in a place I fell in love with, too."

"Just so you know, I would have come to you."

"I found your note."

"So you know," he said. "Where are you now?"

"In an Uber, on the way to the airport. I didn't want to stay at the hotel, so I'll catch the first flight I can find back to Seattle."

"You and conference hotels."

She scoffed. "At least this time I had all my luggage."

"And you *still* wore that T-shirt?"

She laughed again. "God, I love you."

"I love you, too. Hurry up, *agapi mou*."

~~~~~~~~~~~~~~~~~~~~~~~~~~~~~~~~~~~

Having most of her belongings still in boxes in her apartment turned out to be a blessing, since it was easier to organize a shipment for the things she wanted to send to Greece. All Olivia had to do was pack her clothes. The only two things she planned to carry with her in addition to the two large suitcases were two framed pictures—Thalia's painting and the framed poster of *Café Terrace At Night*, which she took off the wall.

By Friday night, she was fully packed and discovered she had gone viral again. This time, by permission. Lynn Michaels had contacted her that morning and asked if they could post her speech on the summit's website.

"Go ahead," Olivia had said. "I don't have anything to hide this time."

"I did you a favor," Daria said that evening when she came to help with the final arrangements. "I showed the video to Tyler. Give it twenty-four hours, and Jeff will be off your back."

She was right. Later that night, Olivia received a text message from Jeff that contained one word, and he had even typed it himself. "*Congratulations*."

"*Thanks*," she typed back.

Daria stayed over and went with Olivia to her parents on Saturday morning to break the news to them.

She started by telling them all about Niko and his family, and how she had fit in there. Olivia knew her parents wouldn't think to look for her speech online, so she showed it to them while the four of them were in the living room of the Duncans' suburban house.

"That's very nice, Livvy," her father said. "They all seem to like your speech. But, what does it mean?"

Olivia pursed her lips and flashed a sad smile at her dad. She had no doubt her mother had understood exactly what it had meant. She turned her eyes to her.

"I don't understand. What will you do there for work?" was Becky's first question. "Do you plan to work as a waitress?"

"I'll continue to help at the taverna whenever I can, but there are jobs there, Mom. I could work in a hotel; they need HR people, too. Maybe there are relevant job openings. And, if not, then there are other things I could do. Think of it as a relocation. Many people relocate. I'm reinventing myself. I'm so much happier there." She moved her gaze back to her father.

"Are you comparing working in a hotel to high-tech?" her mother asked, and Olivia turned to look at her again.

"No, but I've done high-tech and am ready to start something new. I'm comparing happiness with unhappiness, living with the man I love versus living without him, living in a place that makes me want to devour the world every morning versus living in a place that no longer makes me happy. Be glad for me, Mom. And think about it, now you know where your next vacation will be."

"If she moved with Jeff to Boston, it would have been the same. We'd see her on Christmas and maybe once in the summer. I'm sure this could be the same. And Greece is nicer," Jack Duncan told his wife.

~~~~~~~~~~~~~~~~~~~~~~~~~~~~~~~~~

"It went okay," Daria said later when they were back in Olivia's apartment.

"Like removing a Band-Aid; that's the best way to do it," Olivia said. "For them and for me. There's no point in dragging this out. Plus, I can't wait to be back with Niko."

Daria leaned back on Olivia's couch, the one that came with the apartment. "Well, that's your parents, but what about me?"

"I wish you could come with me. I'm gonna miss you so much."

"We'll meet at least twice a year, right?" Daria said.

"We have to." Olivia looked around at the naked walls. Their voices echoed in the almost empty space.

"I might just surprise you someday," Daria said. "You've inspired me. Besides, I'm trying to convince myself that it would be like when you were with Jeff. We didn't meet that often back then."

"But that was because—"

"I couldn't stand Jeff," Daria completed for her, and they both laughed. "The good news is that I already like Niko."

Daria spent the weekend with Olivia and, on Sunday, after they both went to lunch again at Olivia's parents, she drove Olivia to the airport.

"You'll see me before the end of the year, I promise," Daria said when they hugged.

"I'm counting on it."

"Now go! You have someone waiting for you."

"I can't wait. Meeting him was the best thing that has ever happened to me. I can't thank you enough for screwing up that day."

Daria laughed. "You can always count on me."

Chapter 19

Her luggage arrived this time. Though the moment she spotted Niko's face in the crowd, Olivia couldn't care less about anything else.

She ran to him, the wheels of her suitcases barely keeping up with her pace. When she was close enough, she let go of the handles and jumped into his arms. Like the first time she had kissed him, Niko hardly swayed when the brunt of her crashed against him. He caught her in his arms and lifted her, and she wrapped her legs around his waist. All Olivia could hear, smell, and taste was him.

"Miss, your suitcases," someone said in English next to them, forcing them to break their kiss.

"I'm sorry, I'm sorry," Olivia mumbled just as Niko mumbled the same in Greek to the airport uniformed employee who had brought her deserted luggage.

"We're making a scene," she half-whispered, chuckling, her lips still hovering over Niko's. She put her feet back on the floor, but his arms were still around her.

"You're getting used to making scenes, huh?" Niko teased, huffing the words against her lips.

"God, I missed you so much. I can't believe it's only been a week. It feels like a year."

"Come on; I booked us a hotel," he said, letting go of her and grabbing her suitcases.

"We're staying?" she asked, entwining her arm in his. All she knew was that she was with him. She hadn't cared what happened after she had arrived in Athens and left all the rest of the arrangements and planning to him. It was very un-Olivia of her, and she knew it. She reveled in it.

"I usually stay at Cleo's, but I wanted us to have privacy," he said, lowering his voice and inclining his head toward her ear. Just these words were enough to make her burn for him. "And you could see Athens and meet her and Andreas later."

After picking up the framed pictures from the special items counter—"You brought the painting back? And it has a sibling?" Niko had asked—they walked out into the heat of a Greek summer afternoon.

She was so used to Niko having a poison-green convertible that, when they approached a non-descript white rental, she didn't connect the dots.

Niko opened the door for her, but before she climbed into the car, Olivia leaned against it and pulled Niko in for another kiss. "Is it far?" she asked.

"I'm afraid so," he rasped. Then, pulling himself back, he added, "It's in the city center—thirty-minute drive—but you'll love it."

The airport and industrial views turned into urban ones, and then they were soon in the suburbs of Athens.

They talked about the passing week but, as if by a mutual, unspoken agreement, they held back the important things, knowing that there would be a better time for that later. She told him about the reactions that she had received online, about Jeff's text, her conversations with her parents, and her last weekend with Daria. Niko said his week was mostly spent with his brother and sister, and nephew and niece.

"You left the taverna for a whole week?" she asked.

"That's the beauty about a family business— we're a well-oiled machine. Elena runs the show, and everyone knows when and what to do, including watering the plants at the house." Niko sent her a lopsided grin.

It was hard to keep their hands off each other. While Niko had the wheel and stick shift to manage, Olivia had her hands free. She stroked his arm, nape, thigh—anything she could that wouldn't get them into a car accident. They held hands when his right palm wasn't busy with switching gears.

The outskirts of Athens looked just as she had imagined a Mediterranean city would look like. The afternoon sun painted everything in warmer colors, and two prominent points were seen through the car windows.

"That's the Acropolis and that's Lycabettus Hill," Niko pointed.

That accent of his never ceased making her mouth water.

"It's … amazing, for lack of a better description." Olivia wondered how many couples in love had watched the Acropolis in its twenty-five hundred years of existence.

Driving past the Greek parliament and through beautiful boulevards, they entered the Monastiraki neighborhood that was at the foot of one side of the

Acropolis. A combination of ancient and new, bustling and unspoiled, it was like a postcard.

Niko parked the car near a small hotel. The room was already his, so no time was wasted on checking in, which was wonderful because, as soon as the door was closed behind them, Olivia threw her arms around Niko, craving to freely tell him in every possible way how much she loved him. Whispered in two languages, spoken in two voices, or with no words at all, Love, Home, and Niko became synonymous for Olivia.

~~~~~~~~~~~~~~~~~~~~~~~~~~~~~~~

After showering together and not yet willing to leave the room, despite the beautiful evening outside, they ordered room service and ate on the room's balcony. Their view was the neighborhood's vibrant square and the illuminated, majestic Acropolis high above it. The sounds of people talking and music carried over to them with the evening breeze.

"Here's to us, to new beginnings, and to saying *I love you* out loud," Olivia said, clinking Niko's glass with hers.

"And to simpler and better things," Niko added. They clinked their glasses again, then sipped the cool white wine.

"How did you know?" he asked, and she knew exactly what he meant.

"I knew before. I was just too scared to make the decision. My heart knew, but my mind wouldn't let it decide. It was just like you said; once the balance shift was clear, everything became clearer and easier. Did you know it was going to happen?"

"I hoped for it, because I saw it on you. Your face is like the water in the secret cove—so clear you can see everything under it. But I didn't know what would happen until you said it on that stage. Once you went back, anything was possible. I was making plans on asking you, coming to you, something, but then … Cleo thought I was crazy. It was six in the morning here, and I was sitting and watching your video live on my phone. When you said what you said, I jumped up and knocked down a lamp. Almost woke the whole house."

Olivia laughed. "I guess I know what to buy Cleo as a present—a new lamp. I'm so nervous."

"Don't be. They're going to love you. When I told Elena and Kostas that you're coming back to stay, they were happy. And Nina called me five minutes after I hung up with them. She wanted to call you, but I told her it was the middle of the night for you."

"Kostas was happy?" Olivia squinted her eyes in disbelief.

"I know he looks tough—my father was like that, too—but he likes you. If he *didn't* like you, you'd know. Trust me."

~~~~~~~~~~~~~~~~~~~~~~~~~~~

The next day, they spent the morning sightseeing. Niko took her to the gorgeous Plaka neighborhood, and they climbed up to the Acropolis through the white-washed winding alleys of

Anafiotika. It reminded Olivia a lot of the island. The Parthenon on top of the Acropolis left her almost speechless, but her favorite part was the "Porch of the Maidens," with its six draped female figures called caryatids that served as supporting columns for the roof. Her other favorite part was holding Niko's hand, taking selfies with him, chatting, and kissing like a new couple while feeling as if they had always been together.

They met Cleo and her children for lunch in a taverna overlooking another touristic point, the Syntagma square and the Greek Parliament house. The kids were eight and six years old and didn't speak a word in English, but Olivia managed to communicate with them using the few words in Greek that she knew when she gave them the presents she had bought in a gift shop on the way down from the Acropolis.

"I heard I owe you a table lamp," she told Cleo, who looked a lot like Nina, though her hair was shorter and she didn't braid it like Nina always did. She wore rimless glasses and, behind the clear lenses, her eyes shone honey-green like her brother's.

"Just to see Niko like that, I would gladly let him break a few more things," Cleo said, smiling. "I hope you don't mind, but he showed me the video later."

"I don't mind at all," Olivia said.

"We're spending a week in Corfu every summer when most offices are closed here, so I'll be happy to spend more time with you," Cleo told Olivia before they parted.

"I'm looking forward to it," Olivia replied.

Cleo kissed her twice on the cheeks.

Olivia and Niko stopped at the hotel to pick up the painting before continuing to visit Andreas in the afternoon. The night before, she had carefully brought up the idea, and Niko loved it. "He doesn't have a picture of the taverna and would probably love to have this painting. I don't know why I haven't thought about it before," Niko said. "He left Corfu after our parents passed away because he wanted to take the opportunity to live alone and see other places, like healthy men his age do. It wasn't because he had bad memories or anything like that; it's just that here, it's easier to do than in Corfu," he added when Olivia had voiced her concern.

They crossed the city, driving through the wide and beautiful Amalias Avenue. The rented car's windows were open to admit the afternoon breeze and the noise of the Mediterranean capital.

"He doesn't speak English, and he tends to either not speak at all or speak very fast when he's excited. I'll translate," Niko prepared her on the way. "You're going to love him."

The place Andreas was living in was a gated community consisting of houses with a few tenants living with two staff members in each. Those who could work were employed in an employment center. Andreas's paintings were printed on postcards, gift wraps, paper bags, calendars, and other paper products and sold mainly to businesses.

Andreas himself asked Niko to translate this explanation to Olivia when they sat with him in the garden of the house he lived in. Andreas seemed as happy to meet her as Cleo had been earlier.

"I promise to improve my Greek so, when we visit you in the coming months, you and I will be able to converse much more without Niko's translation," Olivia told Andreas in English, and Niko translated. She sat facing Andreas, who was in a wheelchair, holding her hands.

"I have something for you. I hope you'll like it." She then showed him the painting and explained how she came to have it.

"Thank you. I love it. Thalia told me about it, but I've never seen it. Thank you. I will ask to hang it in our living room," Niko translated Andreas's words.

When they left an hour later, Niko grabbed her wrist in the parking lot and pulled her to him, hugging and kissing her. "Andreas loved you. He's very sensitive and has a radar for people. He's not always that comfortable with people he's not familiar with."

"He's great. He looks a lot like you, and the three of you have the same eyes," Olivia said.

That evening, they strolled Monastiraki's streets with its boutiques, tavernas, and tourist attractions.

"This food is great," she told Niko over the dishes they shared in one of the tavernas, "but I miss Elena's cooking."

That night, leaning on her arm, her head supported by her palm, and looking at Niko from above as she loved doing, Olivia stroked his face and chest. "I was thinking about the practical side of things," she opened.

Niko, who was playing with the ash-blonde curls that fell into her face, smiled. "I was wondering when you'd bring that up."

"We jumped headfirst, but there are things we need to decide upon," she said.

"I'll move out of the apartment and into the house with you. I want to wake up with you there every morning. I already checked, and you can work in Greece almost immediately, if it's for an international company. There's some paperwork involved, but it's doable. There are a few international companies represented in Corfu and several international hotel chains. I'm sure they would love to have someone with your experience. I didn't start asking around because I wanted you to choose how and when you want to do this. If you find something you like, you can use my car. I hardly use it. What other practicalities did you have in mind?" He smirked.

"I'm glad I'm not the only practical one." Olivia chuckled and bent to kiss him.

"It's my financial attaché side. Always juggling scenarios."

"I want to see you in one of those suits one day," she teased. Their kiss intensified.

"In it or out of it?" Niko rasped and, holding her by her waist, he flipped them over and was on top of her again. "Take your time deciding," he whispered into her ear before sliding down to kiss her neck and farther down from there.

The view of the green island in a sea of blue made Olivia draw a deep breath, and though it was only the circulated air of the plane, she felt like she was taking in a lungful of the salty fresh sea air.

This time, instead of painfully clenching her heart, the terminal near Corfu Town widened it, and she rushed to the parked green car as if it was an old friend that had been patiently waiting.

"I knew I missed you, I knew I missed this, but being here, I realize it even more," she said on the ride to Aleniki.

Entering the village and driving toward the alley behind the taverna was like coming home. It felt more like that than her ride in an Uber toward her apartment in Seattle.

It was a Wednesday, and the taverna was open. Niko left their luggage at the staircase, and they entered the taverna from the back.

Kostas was at the bar, and he and Niko exchanged a hug and shoulder pats. The large man then turned toward Olivia.

"Welcome, Olivia," he said. "We are happy." It was the longest speech she had heard from him that did not relate to work.

Instead of extending her hand to him, she took a step forward and hugged him. Kostas lingered a second, then squeezed her to him. Drowning in his embrace, her head tilted up to draw air, Olivia noticed that the daily menu on the wall still included English.

In the kitchen, she met Elena, who wiped her hands on her apron and hugged and kissed her, accompanying it with a long sentence in Greek.

"You learn Greek fast, yes?" Elena then said, holding Olivia by her forearms and smiling. "I say before that you here is like salt for Niko."

"Salt?" Olivia asked, thinking that either Elena's English or her own hearing was at fault.

"Salt. Niko has good life, but missing. Like food with no salt. You are salt."

Olivia bit her lower lip as if it could stop her from melting inside. Wordlessly, she hugged Elena again.

Hoping Elena wouldn't notice the wet glint in her eyes, she asked, "How can I help today?"

"No need. Angie come soon."

Niko came in to greet his aunt. He looked over at Olivia and smiled while Elena said something that sounded to Olivia like a congratulation speech.

"Let's get you settled back in," he said after Elena stepped outside.

They took her suitcases and the framed picture to the house, and Olivia opened all the windows to air it out again. While she was spreading a sheet on the bed, Niko embraced her from behind and, before long, they rumpled the sheet until it required a respread later.

"Look what I found," Niko said when she was making them both coffee in the kitchen later. Olivia spun and saw him holding the "*I heart Greece*" T-shirt that she had left with the note.

"Oh, right. I almost forgot about it," she said.

Niko breathed out a laughter. "A small matter now, but I think I would be on a plane to Seattle if I found it before."

"So, it's good that I found your note first or we would pass by each other and be alone on the wrong continent again."

Niko approached her and wrapped his arms around her waist, still holding the shirt. "The continent doesn't matter."

Olivia slid her fingers under his sleeve and caressed the globe tattoo. "It really doesn't."

Chapter 20

In the following days, Olivia had the pleasure of meeting both Nina and Thalia again. Each of them took the opportunity to whisper to her that they had known she would be back. She also helped Niko pack up his apartment and move to the house.

In the mornings or late nights, and some days in both, they sat on the veranda, cuddled in the armchair that still stood there. It was on the veranda that she told him about the two interviews she had scheduled. One of them was for an HR manager position in a large hotel in Corfu Town. "I really want this one. If I get it, I'll finally have a chance to actually manage the human resource and not just consult and advise others how to do it. It will be interesting to practice what I preach."

She got it.

Knowing that employers tend to google candidates' histories, she had told her interviewer in advance about the mishap at the conference but made sure to show her Doreen's recommendation letter, as well as Lynn's.

Now Olivia had a full and real life built in Corfu. A house, a job, a community and, most importantly, the love of her life. Nothing was borrowed, nothing temporary.

Though she missed her parents, brother, and Daria, she knew she would see them soon. Her parents had made plans to visit before the summer was over, and Daria had promised to come again before Christmas.

~~~~~~~~~~~~~~~~~~~~~~~~~~~~~~~~~~~~~~~

But it wasn't just a vacation the Duncans arrived for the following September. Olivia's parents, her brother and his family, as well as Daria and Tyler, whom Daria had announced would be her plus-one, arrived for a wedding that was held on a beach taverna in Paleokastritsa.

"If we do it in our taverna, my family will be working instead of partying," Niko had said when they had discussed the details. True to Olivia's practical self, that discussion had been held only a day after Niko had proposed to her.

"I was thinking of doing this in the cove or on the beach, but to me, this veranda has the most beautiful view with colors that remind me of you— blue, yellow, green," Niko had said one night when they sat in the armchair.

"Doing what?" Olivia had asked, her head leaning on his shoulder.

"This," Niko had replied and, extracting himself from under her and causing her to sit up, he had then knelt at the foot of the armchair, holding a ring with a blue-green sapphire encircled by small diamonds. "Olivia, *tha me pantrefteis*? Will you marry me?"

Olivia's heart had gone from a standstill to a manic thrumming in a matter of seconds. "Niko! Oh, my God! Yes, of course." She had thrown her arms around his neck, and he had held her. "*S'agapo*, Niko," she had whispered in his ear.

"I love you, too," he had said in English. "I hope you like the ring."

"The ring! Yes, I love it," she had said, releasing him and letting him put it on her finger.

He could have asked her to marry him with a plastic ring, and she would have been just as excited. But that ring was just what she would have picked out herself.

~~~~~~~~~~~~~~~~~~~~~~~~~~~~~~

Although the ceremony was held in a nearby church, and the reception in Paleokastritsa, the guests stayed in Aleniki. It was the first time the village had such a large group of tourists staying in it. Olivia's brother's family got the small house for the week, while Olivia stayed with Niko in his former apartment. Her parents spent it in an en-suite with a kitchenette and a patio that they rented from a neighbor, two houses to the left of hers and Niko's house. And Daria and Tyler spent it in another en-suite that usually served as a home to two of the triplets, who, for that week, moved back into their parents' house. Cleo and her family, along with Andreas, stayed with Elena and Kostas, who had a hard time letting them go back to Athens once their one-week stay was over.

"I wish you had let me invite Maria Soltis," Becky Duncan told her daughter on the veranda of the house a day before the wedding. "It's so beautiful and peaceful here, and everyone is so nice. I'm happy for you, Livvy. Niko is a great guy."

~~~~~~~~~~~~~~~~~~~~~~~~~~~~~~~~~~~

In a pearl white dress that she had bought in Corfu Town, and her hair curling down her shoulders, Olivia married Niko. He was in a suit but later took his jacket and tie off, remaining in the white shirt with the sleeves folded up and two top buttons open.

"I'll never be tired of this view," Olivia whispered to him on the beach taverna dance floor, trailing her fingers over his chest.

"You're doing great," Olivia told her parents in one of the intermissions between dances. "You don't have to know the steps here; you just dance. That's the beauty of it."

After the reception and party were over, the newlyweds drove back to Aleniki. When Niko parked the car behind the taverna, Olivia said, "Let's go in, just the two of us, before we go home. This is where it all began for me."

"For me, too. Table thirty-two," Niko said, opening the taverna's back door.

They walked into the quiet, dark space. Olivia turned on the laptop and the speakers that were connected to it, which were used daily to play the music in the taverna. She then picked a song on YouTube.

In her wedding dress, Olivia approached Niko, and they slow-danced to the sound of a Greek song that she could hum in the intimate silence of Teresi

Taverna where, of all days, on one of the worst days of her life, she had come to find him and herself on a green spot in a sea of blue.

OTHER BOOKS IN THE SERIES

Each book in the *Of All Hearts* series is set in another beautiful location and is about finding love in an unexpected place, time, and partner.

Other books in the series include:

"*Of All Places*" – set in Kotor, Montenegro. She's read all about romance but never found love. Will a spontaneous trip to Europe lead her to the love of her life?

★★★★★ "Lily Baines has written the perfect chick-lit, contemporary romance...A wonderfully conceived and written story that flows effortlessly from page one. It leaves you with 'all the feels'." - **The Lit Buzz**

"*Of All People*" – set in Rimini, Italy. Can mending a derelict hotel help mend two lonely hearts?

★★★★★ "Lily Baines is a wonderful romance writer who is able to whisk her readers away from everyday life…Her characters and the development of their relationships are captivating…Lily can be trusted for a delightfully entertaining romance with a happily-ever-after...Her locations are stunning and off the beaten path. Her writing is enticing and I keep adding them to my list of places to visit someday." - **The Lit Buzz**

ABOUT THE AUTHOR

Lily Baines is a mother, wife, and author, and the order to this changes depending on the day. For 20 years she worked in Human Resources, mostly in the high-tech industry, but kept writing to maintain her sanity and flow of creative juices. In the past year, Lily is dedicating her time to her 3 children, husband, family dog, bottomless laundry basket, full kitchen sink, and her writing.

Lily's first book, "*A Case Of Longing*", a romantic suspense novel, was published in March of 2020. Since then, she published three more novels in the "*Of All Hearts*" series.

Lily is always happy to connect through her Facebook page (www.facebook.com/lilybainesauthor). On her site (www.lilybaines.com) you'll find bonus reads, extra epilogues, deleted chapters, free novellas, as well as updates on life, writing, and new releases. Don't hesitate to reach out and join the fun!

ACKNOWLEDGMENT

None of my books would have been written without the support and love of my mother, husband, children, and best friends (a term which includes not just my besties but also my brothers and sisters-in-law). It takes a village to nurture and inject confidence into this author.

This book wouldn't have been what it is without my editor, Kristin Campbell from C&D Editing, and my cover artist, Melinda: http://coveredbymelinda.com/

Printed in Great Britain
by Amazon

72838488R00154